AN ADRIAN WEST THRILLER

THE EXCALIBUR DECEPTION

L.D. GOFFIGAN

Copyright © 2022 by L.D. Goffigan

All rights reserved.

This book or any portion thereof may not be reproduced, or stored in a retrieval system, or transmitted in any form or by any means, electronic, mechanical, photocopying, recording, or otherwise, without the express written permission of the publisher.

ldgoffiganbooks.com

This is a work of fiction. Names, characters, organizations, places, events, and incidents are either products of the author's imagination or used fictitiously.

Printed in the United States of America

Paperback ISBN: 979-8-9902344-1-3

Cover Design by Mibl Art

PROLOGUE

Southern Britannia
522 CE

He should have known that peace would not last.

Ambrosius Aurelanius watched from his vantage point atop the hill that looked over the ancient harbor as the Saxon barbarians swarmed over the lands he and his brave men had long fought for.

It had been over twenty winters since the battle of Badon, when he'd led his army to a decisive victory against the Saxons, sending legions of the barbarians to their gods, just as they had slaughtered his own parents when he was just a boy.

Since that day, the lands of southern Britannia had maintained a fragile peace, a peace its people had enjoyed when the legions of Rome protected these lands.

Yet during those years of peace, he had always sensed the looming barbarian threat, a persistent, threatening whisper in the back of his mind. He knew the barbarians were merely a slumbering dragon; it was only a matter of time before it awakened, roaring to life, threatening to consume everything in its path.

He should have been more prepared for this day. Over the years, he'd kept his men trained, made certain they were always on sharp alert, even sending out scouting parties to survey the shores should the slumbering beast make another attempt on their lands.

With each winter that passed without another incursion, with another blessed peace, he had grown more complacent. He had wed a woman he loved, a golden-haired beauty called Laelia, who had borne him three sons who were now men.

He had settled into living his life in the lands that he'd fought all those years ago to protect. Watching his sons grow from babes to men, attending local festivals honoring the old gods as the seasons changed, walking along the shore with his hand entwined in Laelia's, the whisper of the summer's breeze surrounding them.

And now that peace was shattered. Ambrosius had awoken to a scout entering his bedchamber, warning him that he'd spotted Saxon ships approaching.

He'd known in that moment what he must do, a heaviness settling over his heart.

Ambrosius had sent his family away, to the *colonia* of Brittany, where other Britons of their ilk had settled. His wife and sons had refused at first, his sons wanting to stay and fight, but he had insisted, lying to them and telling them he would join them once he'd driven back the Saxons. He could still feel the wetness of his Laelia's tears against his tunic, begging him to come back to her, alive. It was as if she knew what his true fate would be.

He was an older man now, in his fifty-third winter. His strength was not what it once was, when he was the great general who'd defeated the Saxons. Despite what he'd told his family, he would not join his men in this fight, though he knew the Saxons would look for him. He was known among them, his name a curse on their lips.

He could not risk falling into enemy hands, not with what he knew. There was too much at stake, too much that lay on the precipice. When he'd told his brethren what he planned to do, no one had protested. They knew the importance of the secret that he alone held.

Ambrosius took one last look at his men below, who were bravely fighting the advancing Saxons, before turning to do something he'd never once done in his life.

Walk away from battle.

It took everything in Ambrosius' power to not follow his men, to continue the fight, but what he had to do was far more important. He reminded himself that he was protecting the people, not just of this land, winning all future battles that were to come—even if this particular one were to be lost. Still, he had to force himself to make his descent down the hill, making his way to the open fields, toward the forest that clung to their edge.

He kept walking until he reached the forest, not stopping until he found an open grove. Such groves were once sacred to the druids, from whom he was partially descended. It was they who had first guarded the secret that he and a select few of his brethren now guarded with their lives.

A secret that he must now give his life for.

Ambrosius reached the shadow of an ancient, gnarled oak tree, the one where he'd told his brothers they could find him when the time came.

He sank to his knees beneath the tree and unsheathed his sword. Though he knew it was sacrilege, he whispered a prayer to the old gods, the ones worshipped by his druid ancestors, the ones who came before the Christ child.

Ambrosius closed his eyes and sank his sword into his belly.

The pain was sharp and sudden, but he allowed himself to feel it, to claim him with its iron grip. He felt his body sink to the ground, watching as the world faded around him.

The secret of the ancients will die with me and my brethren, he thought, as he drew his last, ragged breath.

CHAPTER 1

Two Weeks Ago
Ten Miles East of Dorset, England
4:07 A.M.

Rhys Sumner cranked up the music on his iPhone, trying to fight past the fatigue weighing his eyes down as he focused on the road ahead.

This wasn't his usual route, but he'd picked up the extra shift because he needed the money. *Urgent, high-profile transfer,* his boss had told him, explaining why it had to take place so bloody early in the morning. All Rhys knew was that he was driving artifacts from a dig site in Dorset to the British Museum in London.

Rhys personally didn't see what the big deal was. He'd never understood the appeal in old shite that long-dead people had once used. Who bloody cared?

But it was a job. He was already late on his rent, and his landlord was on him. If he didn't shape up, Molly, his girlfriend, was certain to leave him, insisting he needed a proper job if they were to continue. She didn't take his music seriously, didn't understand that it took time to make money from it.

Rhys scowled, cranking up the music even louder. He was listening to classic Led Zeppelin, a band whose greatness he aspired to have his own band rise to. His eyes drooped again, and he lowered the window, hoping the wind whipping by would keep him alert. He just needed to focus on getting through the long drive to London. Perhaps having several post-dinner drinks with his bandmates at the pub the evening prior wasn't the wisest thing to do. Besides his fatigue, his head pounded with a persistent hangover.

As the crescendo of the chorus to "Stairway to Heaven" rose, a figure appeared directly in the road in front of him.

Startled, Rhys slammed on the brakes, sending the van screeching to a halt.

Wide awake now, adrenaline coursing through his veins, Rhys gripped the steering wheel, glaring at the man who stood in the middle of the road before him. He wore a long, hooded coat, so Rhys couldn't make out his features.

Once his shock subsided, anger replaced it. What the hell was this wanker doing? He rolled his window down farther to shout at him, but two dark

SUVs suddenly pulled up to a screeching halt alongside his van. Several men emerged, sporting large guns that looked like they belonged in an action film, aiming them directly at him.

Terror gripped Rhys as the hooded man stepped forward, approaching the side of his van. He could now see that the man was young, not much older than he was, with cold green eyes that seemed to look right through him.

"Get out," the man said simply. His accent was posh, moneyed; he sounded like a member of the royal family. He certainly didn't sound like someone who would randomly stand in the middle of the road at four in the morning.

Fear forced Rhys to move. He opened the door, stumbling out of the van. He didn't realize his hands were shaking until he raised them, terror threatening to swallow him whole.

"Please," Rhys said. "I—"

He never got to finish his sentence. Never saw the flash of a pistol or heard the gunshot.

There was only the splintering pain in his chest, surprise, horror... and then nothing.

DECLAN WATCHED as the young driver slumped to the ground before him, dead, his eyes still wide open in surprise, Led Zeppelin blaring from the van.

He whirled to see Wolfe, the mercenary who'd

emerged from the SUV, calmly putting away his pistol.

Wolfe was a hulking, intimidating man who towered over Declan's six-foot-three frame. He lived up to his moniker, even the other mercenaries seemed afraid of him. His dark eyes met Declan's, a silent challenge in their depths.

"You didn't have to kill him," Declan said, keeping his voice steady, though an array of emotions flooded him—anger, disbelief, guilt. "He was going to cooperate."

"The orders were no witnesses," Wolfe replied.

Declan clenched his fists at his sides, taking a shuddering breath to calm himself, trying not to think of the fear in the driver's eyes as he'd died. The driver had to be around his age.

He forced himself to turn away from the driver's body. There was nothing he could do now. He forced aside his conflicting emotions, watching as one mercenary expertly removed the van's tracker that was connected to the battery. Once he'd disconnected it, Declan entered the van, sliding into the driver's seat.

The mercenaries immediately got into their SUVs to follow him, except for the two who rushed forward to move the driver's body.

Declan averted his eyes from the sight, clearing his mind and focusing on the road as he drove for several more kilometers before taking a side road to turn off the motorway, driving far enough to be out of view of any passing car.

Only then did he pull over and climb out, unlocking the back doors of the van. His hungry eyes took in the bagged and boxed artifacts from the dig site, carefully sealed and catalogued. He flipped on the van's inner light, searching among the packages for the particular one he was looking for.

He froze when his gaze landed upon it. A box labeled simply: *Iron sword. Dating pending.*

It was so much more than a sword. Heart hammering, he reached for the box, using a box cutter from his pocket to carefully open it.

Inside was what he'd been looking for . . . what so many had been looking for. *The* sword. He held it for several long moments, reverent, until Wolfe stated, "We should keep going."

Declan tried not to flinch; he didn't realize that Wolfe was standing right behind him.

He gritted his teeth, irritated that Wolfe had interrupted this moment. But Wolfe was right. They still had a long drive, and it wouldn't take long for the museum to realize their shipment hadn't arrived.

And he was eager to share the sword with the person who would appreciate it the most . . . the leader of the brotherhood. He would see Declan's dedication.

Declan cradled the box in his arms as he made his way back to the driver's seat. He wouldn't let it out of his sight.

Its power was too significant to risk losing.

CHAPTER 2

Today
New Scotland Yard - Art and Antiques Unit
London, England
10:32 A.M.

"A couple of months ago, in the remote hills of Dorset, a young boy stumbled upon a hoard of artifacts from sub-Roman era Britain," Detective Constable Jack Stevens said. As he spoke, he gestured to the slide projected onto the wall.

Adrian West and her partner, Nick Harper, took in the images on the slide. The artifacts consisted of coins and weapons, including javelins, daggers, and several shields.

"The dig continued for several weeks, and the site was fully excavated. But the van transporting the artifacts was stolen and its tracker turned off. The driver was found dead not far off the M3 motorway. He was shot point-blank and dragged off the road."

Stevens flipped the slide to several grisly photographs of a crime scene: the dead young driver, his eyes wide and unseeing.

"We were contacted straight away. Homicide is working the case of the driver while we're on the artifacts. Homicide believes his murder is cut and dry, and we're in agreement. He was just an unlucky bloke who happened to be transporting valuable artifacts, and the thieves wanted him out of the way. We find the thieves, we find the murderer."

Stevens switched to another slide. It featured an iron sword with an intricately designed hilt. The handle of the sword resembled a claw, while the hilt's end was shaped like a crown. The blade of the sword was iron, and a copper-alloy material covered the hilt.

"We believe the key to the theft is this item. This is the item the excavators are the most concerned with. Unlike the other artifacts, it dates back to an earlier time period—the late Iron Age, prior to the Roman invasion. But it was buried alongside all the other artifacts, so it was used at the same time. Given its dating and the rarity of the materials used, that makes it even more valuable than the other artifacts. In fact, some of the excavators have nicknamed the sword Excalibur."

Nick raised his eyebrows. "Excalibur? As in King Arthur?"

"The one and only," Stevens said with a grin.

"Why?" Adrian asked. "What does this artifact have to do with a mythological sword?"

"Not everyone thinks Excalibur is mythological," Stevens said, shaking his head. "For those who believe in a historical Arthur, he lived around the time of Rome's fall, fighting off Saxon invaders. This very unique sword is from that time period."

"That's a lot of speculation," Nick said, and Adrian had to agree. She had never given the Arthurian story much thought, but held the view of most historians, that he was purely a legendary character. Calling the sword "Excalibur" certainly gave this find an aura of excitement, but that didn't mean it was linked to any sort of hard historical truth. Cases like these were solved with facts, and the facts were that someone had stolen these artifacts and murdered an innocent man.

"Can you click back to the photos of the crime scene?" she asked.

Stevens obliged, though she could tell he was itching to extrapolate on the whole Excalibur notion. Adrian leaned forward, studying the open field that the killer had dragged the driver's body to, along with the tire tracks.

She mentally went over the facts of the murder and subsequent theft of the artifacts in her head. The unfortunate driver was surrounded at around four in the morning by someone who knew his route and knew to disable the van's tracker. The multiple tire tracks indicated other cars, far more than should be needed to take out a simple delivery van to the British Museum.

"What are you thinking?" Nick asked.

"These were professionals. Definitely an inside job," she said. "They knew the driver's route and what he had with him."

"We've questioned everyone who worked on the dig, and the department who was going to take in the artifacts at the British Museum," Stevens said. "Everyone's alibi checks out."

"Someone's lying," Adrian said bluntly. "We need to talk to them again."

Stevens bristled, but Nick nodded his agreement. "You brought us in to assist, Jack. It can't hurt for us to re-interview people."

Stevens offered a reluctant nod. "I'll get you the log of our interviews."

"Who was the lead on the dig?" Adrian asked.

"Doctor Sorcha Manning."

12:15 P.M.

ADRIAN AND NICK entered the massive lobby of the British Museum known as the Queen Elizabeth II Great Court, its overhead spiral glass roof casting crisscrossing shadows onto the museum floor.

Located in central London, the British Museum was one of the largest museums in the world, with millions of works filling its over two hundred thousand square feet, including famous works such as the Rosetta Stone and the Parthenon sculptures. Adrian had always loved coming to this museum, one of many she'd visited with her professor father and her mother when she was younger, instilling in her an early love of history.

Now, as she made her way toward the Department of Britain, Europe and Prehistory with Nick, she couldn't believe that just a few days ago she'd been at New York University, where she was a consulting lecturer and professor of ancient languages and manuscripts. It was on the heels of her discovery of Cleopatra's tomb—and treasure—something that had briefly made her a minor celebrity. The attention had thankfully waned, with the focus now on the discovery itself, which Adrian was relieved for.

Yet her experience in Egypt, during which she and Nick had rescued her friend and colleague Sebastian Rossi from a nefarious group intent on finding Cleopatra's tomb, had reawakened something that had lain dormant since she'd left law enforcement to enter academia. The hunger to solve mysteries, to save lives in doing so . . . something that was personal for her, given the disappearance of her father over ten years ago. So when Nick had asked her to consult on this case, she hadn't hesitated to say yes.

She'd taken a leave of absence from the university and flown to England with Nick. Both Jeremy

Briggs, Nick's boss at FBI's Art Crimes division, and Nick, were friendly with the small team of detectives who worked in the Art and Antiques Unit at New Scotland Yard, having worked jointly on a case together several years before. They'd asked for assistance with the high-profile theft; Adrian suspected that Nick's minor celebrity after the discovery of Cleopatra's tomb had prompted the request.

"How does it feel so far? To be back in the thick of it?" Nick asked as they made their way through the bustling crowds of the museum.

"Ask me in a few days," she replied dryly. "By then, I might be missing my students."

"I don't know about that, West," he said with a wink. "Maybe you're right back where you belong."

Adrian only returned his smile, though she couldn't deny how right it felt to be back in the field.

When they reached the Department of Britain, Europe and Prehistory, a young, perky curator's assistant led them to Doctor Sorcha Manning's office, where she came out to greet them.

Manning was younger than Adrian had expected, no older than her late twenties or early thirties, with auburn hair and deep-green eyes that seemed to linger on Nick, which sent a ripple of irritation through Adrian. But Manning's expression hardened when Nick flashed his credentials, telling her they were here to ask her about the stolen artifacts.

"I spoke with the police already," she said shortly. "I don't know what else I can tell you."

"We think what happened was an inside job. Someone knew the route the van was taking and when to intercept it. Do you know of anyone who would have an interest in such a find?" Adrian asked.

She didn't miss the shutter that fell over Manning's eyes, and the brief pause, before she said, "No. Again, the police asked me these questions already."

Adrian studied her for a long moment. Manning was clearly hiding something. Before she could press her, Nick gave Manning a charming smile—which again irritated Adrian—and said politely, "OK. Just thought we'd check. If you think of anything, please don't hesitate to reach out."

Adrian suppressed her irritation until they were outside of the museum.

"Why'd you do that? I had a lot more to ask her. You saw she was hiding something."

"Yes, and as a wise woman once told me, peppering her with more questions she doesn't want to answer won't make her open up. We can have Vince run a background check on her, and if anything comes up, we can use that as leverage when we go talk to her again," Nick said.

Adrian sighed, giving him a nod. He was referring to Adrian's insistence in the past that it was no use trying to get information out of a stubborn suspect. It was best to use some sort of leverage instead.

Vincent Foranelli was the "tech whiz" whom he worked with at the FBI's Art Crimes unit. Now back in DC, he'd helped them significantly on the Cleopatra case when he was stationed in Rome with Nick. Adrian knew he was more than capable of digging up dirt on Sorcha Manning if there was any.

Manning simply didn't want to talk about whatever she knew, which perplexed Adrian. As lead archaeologist on the dig, wouldn't she want everything that could possibly be done to find the missing artifacts?

What are you hiding, Doctor Manning?

CHAPTER 3

12:30 P.M.

Doctor Sorcha Manning watched the handsome American federal agent and his partner leave, unease prickling at her spine. She'd thought that after talking to the detectives from Scotland Yard that would be the end of it. But if they had sent American reinforcements...

Panic swelled within her as she thought of all that was at stake. The less law enforcement agents who were on this, the better. She leaned on her desk, clenching her fists in her lap and taking several deep breaths to calm herself.

"All right, Sorcha?" her assistant, Deb, asked, popping her head into her office.

Sorcha looked up and forced a polite smile. "Yes. Just going to go for a coffee. I'll be back in time for the afternoon meeting."

Her assistant's face softened with concern.

"Take your time. They'll find them, Sorch. We all know how hard you worked on the dig."

Guilt splintered through her at Deb's concern. *If only she knew the truth.* Sorcha forced another smile and headed out.

The museum usually brought her peace; she had fond memories of coming here with her family as a child. It was walking through these halls as a young girl that she'd decided one day she would work here, bringing the past alive for visitors from all over the world. During her grad school days, she'd even come to the museum for leisure, just walking through the various rooms, and taking in her favorite exhibits. But today, everything about the museum felt... oppressive.

She needed air.

Once she left the museum and was a safe distance away, she took out her phone and placed a call.

"I need you to keep an eye on two people—American federal agents. We need to make certain they don't get too close."

Conwyth Estate
Scottish Highlands
2:15 P.M.

CONWYTH ESTATE WAS a sprawling manor of twenty-five rooms nestled deep in the Scottish

Highlands, covering roughly one hundred acres of land.

The estate had originally been built in the fourteenth century as a small manor and gradually added on to and refurbished over time. It had fallen largely into disuse during the eighteenth century, until a series of private owners purchased it, beginning in the late nineteenth century.

Declan had spent a part of his childhood here, but it had never felt like home with its ornate rooms, sprawling passages and corridors . . . it was more like a museum. He'd preferred the smaller townhome he'd shared with his parents and sister just outside of London.

Pain flared in his chest at the thought of his family, and his steps faltered. The grief from his parents' death still lingered, casting a shadow on all the happy memories he had of them. He reminded himself that he was doing all of this for their memory . . . for their family line. He forced himself to continue down the ornate main corridor that led to one of the manor's several grand studies.

Wolfe stood at the entrance to the study, giving him a cold smile as he gestured for him to enter. Declan froze at the sight of him, recalling how easily he'd dispatched that driver.

At first, he didn't know why mercenaries such as Wolfe had to work with the brotherhood. The leader had simply told Declan that they wouldn't hesitate to do what must be done. A chill crept up his spine as he now understood exactly what that meant.

Averting his gaze from Wolfe's cold one, he entered the study. Inside, several men were gathered around the leader of the brotherhood, Grant Macleod, who leaned against the desk, his arms folded, his cool gray gaze trained on Declan. Declan's eyes drifted past him to the sword, which casually rested on the desk behind him.

Declan froze, looking back up at Grant. He should have been looking at him with pride, congratulating him for finding an item that the brotherhood had been seeking for many years. Instead, his demeanor was frosty.

"Our experts don't believe this is the right sword," Grant said in greeting.

Declan stiffened in surprise, his eyes going to the men surrounding Grant. They must be his so called "experts." His mouth tightened. "That sword is the right one," he insisted.

Grant's eyes narrowed. Usually Declan would falter under such a withering look, but he held his ground. "Are you telling me our experts are wrong?"

"I'm telling you your experts are wrong."

Though Grant glared at him, Declan could have sworn he saw a hint of admiration in his gaze. It annoyed Declan how much it pleased him to see just that hint of admiration. But there had always been that part of him that wanted—needed—Grant's approval.

"And why do you think that?" Grant pressed.

"The brotherhood's archives describe the type of swords we should be looking for. The dating, the materials and design of this sword match their description," Declan said. "That's why I wanted to recover it as soon as I learned of its discovery."

"There is no message, no code, nothing on it to indicate that this is the right sword," one man to Grant's right said, glaring at Declan. "If there were, we would have found it by now."

"It's the right sword," Declan repeated. He may not be a seasoned historian like these men were, but something in his gut told him that the sword he'd recovered was one of the swords the brotherhood had long been looking for.

The man turned to Grant with a scowl, no doubt prepared to argue, but Grant held up his hand, his gaze still trained on Declan.

"Let's keep looking at the sword for now. Perhaps there's something we missed," Grant said finally, to Declan's relief and surprise. "If I need you for anything else, Declan, I'll send for you."

It was a not-so-subtle dismissal. Declan bristled, but turned to leave, deciding it would be wise to choose his battles. He'd just won one.

Just as he reached the door, Grant's voice stopped him.

"Sorcha."

Just her name on Grant's lips made icy dread flood Declan's body, and he turned. Grant was studying him closely. "She's not going to be a problem, is she?"

"No," Declan said, trying to keep his voice steady, though fear surged through his body. "Of course not."

"Good," Grant said, giving him a frosty smile. "Let's hope she continues not to be."

CHAPTER 4

London, England
7:12 P.M.

"So," Stevens said, his tone teasing, "I couldn't help but notice some skepticism from both of you when I mentioned the Excalibur of legend."

Nick let out a playful groan while at his side, Adrian just gave Stevens a wary smile.

Nick, Adrian, Stevens, and the two other detectives from the Art and Antiques Unit—Detective Constables Sara Hawthorne and Mark Goode—were gathered at a local pub around the corner from New Scotland Yard.

He and Adrian had spent the rest of the day re-interviewing people who the unit had already spoken to, with no luck. No one was as cagey as Doctor Manning had been, simply answering their questions the same as they had answered the local detectives. No one came off as remotely suspicious. Nick had noticed that even Adrian's sharp eye had detected no deception.

After the final interview, when he and Adrian had returned to Scotland Yard, Stevens must have detected the defeat in their eyes and suggested that they partake in a post-work tradition and enjoy a pint with them at the pub that he and other detectives frequented.

"I've always considered the whole Arthur thing a myth," Adrian said with a shrug. "I believe the thieves who stole the artifacts—especially the sword—were after them for their value."

"Cheers," Goode said, raising his beer in Adrian's direction. "I think the exact same thing. The whole Arthur thing is bollocks."

"I'd have to disagree with both of you," Hawthorne said, shaking her head. "I think beneath most legends, there is *some* truth."

"And you?" Stevens asked Nick. "Not to put you on the spot, mate."

"Ah, but you just did," Nick returned with a grin. "I don't think there's a historical Arthur in the sense that there was a Lancelot, round table, lady of the lake, and all that. But I think he was based on someone."

"I'm taking that for our team," Stevens said with a chuckle. "I absolutely think there's an Arthur—but I'm biased," he admitted with a grin. "My father was a history nut, loved old myths and legends, but Arthur is one he insisted was real."

"On what basis?" Adrian asked, raising her eyebrows. Nick knew that facial expression well. It was her skeptical look.

"Please don't get him started," Hawthorne pleaded.

"Oh, it's too late for that," Stevens said, his eyes twinkling as he turned to focus on Adrian. "We know the story of Arthur because of Geoffrey of Monmouth, an English cleric writing in medieval times, hence Arthur is portrayed as a medieval king ruling over medieval lands—with a medieval sword. That's what most people think of when they think of King Arthur. In reality, Geoffrey's sources were from much earlier, including sub-Roman Britain, the time period right after the Romans left the British Isles."

Hawthorne made a snoring sound; Stevens shot her a playful glare and continued.

"Now, Rome had been stationed in Britain for centuries, giving it a period of relative stability. But once it fell and its legions sent back to the mainland to fight invading barbarian armies, Britain was largely left to fend off invaders on its own, from Saxons to Angles to Jutes. Once Rome fled, the Saxon armies in particular made significant incursions onto the British Isles and would eventually establish early British kingdoms. But there was *someone* who held off the Saxons for a generation or two. The Saxons temporarily retreated, and Britain, for a time at least, had another period of stability. This is when the so-called 'Camelot' period happened. That 'someone' who fought off the Saxons could have very well been the Arthur of legend."

"That's not conclusive evidence," Adrian said, shaking her head. "That could have been just a great leader—or *leaders*."

"OK," Stevens said, holding up his hand, "I'll give you that. But how about this? The name Arthur itself. It's a Roman name—well, Artorius is. In the sixth century, Roman names had basically dissipated and returned to their Celtic roots on the British Isles. Yet, mysteriously, there was a revival of the name with *several* Arthurs on record in royal houses. Just like today, names were often given to children based on famous figures. So I think it's fair to say that there was *someone* who these royal titles were named after in recent memory. It's not farfetched to assume they were named after the same Arthur who held the Saxons off the isles for a time."

"That's . . . compelling," Adrian said, giving him a grudging nod. "Still speculative, though."

"I forget your partner is also a historian," Stevens said to Nick with a playful groan. "Academic historians tend to be hardcore Arthur skeptics."

"Guilty," Adrian said with a grin. "We just want firm evidence before coming to firm conclusions."

"Does Doctor Manning believe Arthur was real?" Nick asked, bringing the subject back to

Sorcha Manning. "We didn't find her very forthcoming," he added. "How was she when you guys questioned her?"

"Really?" Stevens asked, looking genuinely surprised. "She was nothing but forthcoming with us. We didn't discuss the legend of Arthur much; she was just focused on helping us find the artifacts. Told us everything we wanted to know. Offered to be on call if we needed anything else."

"We checked her alibi, just like everyone else," Hawthorne added. "It checks out."

Nick and Adrian exchanged a glance. Nick could tell by the look on her face that she wasn't buying it; neither of them were.

Stevens's phone chimed, and he looked down at it with a grimace.

"That's the wife. I *may* have told her I'd be home an hour ago."

He bid them a good night; Goode and Hawthorne also took their leave. Nick hadn't missed the secret glances the two detectives had shared during their evening out. Now they seemed to go out of their way to keep their distance from each other as they left the pub. He stifled a smirk; they were doing a piss-poor job of hiding their obvious relationship.

His gaze slid to Adrian, who took a sip of her beer, looking deep in thought. He and Adrian had definitely danced close to the line between friendship and romantic relationship, sharing their one and only kiss years ago when they were still partners. But after Adrian left the bureau to work in academia and they'd lost touch, their friendship had become distant, only reigniting during their time in Egypt.

Now, it was as if no time had gone by at all, and they'd slipped back into their old camaraderie with ease, even though he could feel the tug of attraction at the edge of their renewed friendship. He'd not missed the spark of interest in Manning's eyes before he'd revealed he was with the FBI, and he'd also not missed Adrian's irritation at the interest, something that he couldn't help but admit pleased him.

"We could be wrong about Manning," Adrian said, breaking his train of thought as she set down her beer. "But my gut . . ."

"I feel the same way," he said with a sigh. "Let's see what Vince comes up with. Hopefully that'll give us some insight."

Nick paid their tab, and they headed out of the pub, making their way back to their hotel.

It was an unseasonably cool night for late spring, but the streets were still teeming with life, tourists and locals alike stumbling to and from the various pubs.

Adrian abruptly stopped. She turned, reaching up to embrace him, and heat flared within him. Heat that turned to alarm when she spoke, her mouth close to his ear.

"We're being followed."

CHAPTER 5

Nick stiffened against her in alarm. Adrian's pulse fluttered wildly, and not just because of Nick's close proximity.

Adrian had sensed something was off ever since they'd rounded the corner after leaving the pub. She'd brushed off the feeling—until she'd glimpsed the shadow of a man a half block behind, trailing them.

Nick reacted quickly, putting his arms around her, keeping up the pretext that they were an affectionate couple as they continued down the street, careful to keep their pace steady. He leaned down to speak into her ear, keeping his voice low.

"Let's get him to a place where we can corner him."

Adrian nodded her agreement, and they kept walking. Now that she knew they were being followed, it was all she could sense and feel. Her pulse remained erratic, and the hairs on the back of her neck were standing at attention.

Nick was armed, but she wasn't. What if there were others with this man? What did he want? Why was he following them?

She took a breath to calm herself, making herself keep her pace steady with Nick's long strides. Nick gave her a look as they turned onto an empty side street that ended in a dead end, and she gave him a subtle nod. As soon as they made their way halfway down the street—

They both whirled. Their pursuer, a man with a shaved bald head and a tall, hulking form, froze momentarily before turning and darting away.

Adrian and Nick raced after him as he dashed down the side street, heading toward a busy thoroughfare.

Whoever he was, he was damn good at running, outpacing even Nick's long strides. He darted into the middle of the thoroughfare, ignoring honking cars and screeching horns as he weaved around them.

By the time Adrian and Nick made it across the busy thoroughfare, he was nowhere to be seen.

9:45 P.M.

"I'm not saying this isn't significant. I'm just saying we don't have much to go on," Stevens said.

Adrian and Nick stood opposite Stevens in the bullpen area of the Art and Antiques unit of Scotland Yard. They'd called Stevens shortly after losing their pursuer; he'd helped them file an official report.

Still, he clearly had his doubts.

"And we don't know for sure if this guy is related to *this* case," Stevens continued. "Aren't you two still known because of the whole Cleopatra thing?"

"He wasn't a photographer trying to take our picture," Adrian said tightly.

Stevens held up his hands. "Apologies. I just want to make sure we're dedicating resources to the right things."

"Jack, we need to find this guy. I don't think it's a coincidence that we're followed on the same day we start interviewing people about the theft," Nick said, looking just as irritated as she felt.

"OK. I'll have an APB sent out and follow up on it," Stevens said. "Will you two be all right at the hotel? Should we put an officer on you?"

"We'll be fine," Nick said.

"Let me know if anything changes. I'm a phone call away," Stevens said.

Nick's phone rang as they headed out of Scotland Yard. He glanced down at his phone. "It's Vince," he said, and answered, putting it on speaker. "Vince, my boy. What do you have?"

"Not a whole lot, I'm afraid. Doctor Sorcha Manning is everything she appears to be. No criminal background, no suspicious financial transactions. Esteemed education, attended Oxford and Cambridge, where she got her doctorate in early medieval British history. There's some tragedy in her past; her parents died years ago in a car accident, both historians as well. She seems to have family money. Her mother came from a wealthy family. She's clean as a whistle."

Adrian deflated, and Nick heaved a sigh. "OK, Vince. Thanks."

"Is it possible he missed something?" she asked after Nick hung up.

"Vince is the best there is. If she's hiding something significant, she's doing a damn good job of it. Doctor Manning may just be a regular, boring old archaeologist—albeit a cagey one."

Adrian shook her head. This convinced her even more that Manning wasn't who she seemed . . . she was just very good at hiding it. She had the instinctive feeling that whatever it was had to do with the missing artifacts.

And she was determined to find out exactly what it was.

～

London, England
10:07 A.M.

ADRIAN SAT in her parked rental car, her gaze trained on Sorcha Manning as she stepped out of the British Museum.

When they'd returned to the hotel the previous night, she'd told Nick that she wanted to review details of the artifacts with a local historian while he carried out the last of the interviews. This was a lie, but she only felt a little guilty about it.

Instead, she was following Manning, hoping that in doing so, she could uncover *something* about what the other woman was hiding.

It was a necessary lie. Adrian was just a consultant on this case, and officially everything they did was Nick's call. She knew he wouldn't approve of her field trip, especially given what they'd learned from Vince had basically put them at a dead end with Manning.

But Adrian had no choice. It would do no good to question Manning again; she had no interest in opening up to them, and if they approached her, Adrian wouldn't be surprised if she turned hostile. This was the best way to find out something about the cagey archaeologist . . . or at least that's what Adrian hoped.

She watched as Manning hailed a cab and slipped inside. Adrian started up her car and followed, staying two cars back. She followed the cab through the bustling morning London traffic until it stopped at a private townhome in the upscale Kensington neighborhood.

Adrian pulled over at the far end of the street as

Manning left the cab and entered the home. She took out her phone and snapped a picture of the address, sending it to Vince to follow up on. She would have to deal with his questions later.

Adrian lowered her phone, keeping her gaze trained on the house. It had been years since she'd performed any kind of surveillance, and she'd forgotten how utterly boring it was, most of the time panning out to nothing. She hoped this time would be different.

She ended up waiting two hours until Manning exited the house. Adrian straightened in her seat, keeping her gaze trained on Manning as she turned to head down the street, her brow furrowed and expression troubled, when the sound of gunfire suddenly rang out, exploding into the air.

Passersby screamed as Manning slumped to the ground.

CHAPTER 6

Adrian's reaction was instant.

She started the car and swerved out of her parking spot, maneuvering the car in a near three-hundred-sixty-degree turn on the narrow, empty street, screeching to a stop alongside Manning.

To her relief, she could see that Manning was still breathing but playing dead, curled up into a protective ball on the sidewalk.

Adrian leaned over and pushed open the passenger side door. "Get in!" she shouted.

At the sound of her voice, Manning looked up, wild-eyed and terrified. She hesitated—but only for a millisecond—before getting up and crawling into the car, staying crouched low as Adrian sped away.

Adrian scanned the side and rearview mirrors as she sped down the narrow street before taking an abrupt turn onto Kensington High Street, ignoring the irritated honks of other drivers . . . but no one pursued them.

"Who was that?" Adrian demanded, keeping her eyes on the road.

"I—I don't know," Manning stammered.

Adrian gritted her teeth in frustration. Even after she'd rescued her from a damn shooter, Manning was still lying to her. "Now is the time to be truthful with me. Who the hell was shooting at you?"

"I don't know," Manning repeated. She cautiously straightened in her seat after taking a hesitant look at their surroundings before glaring at Adrian with narrowed eyes. "Were you following me?"

"If I was, it was lucky for you," Adrian said, deciding it was best to not directly answer. "I just saved your ass. We need to tell the police about this. I'm taking you to Scotland Yard."

"No! Look, I'm grateful for what you did back there, but you can let me out now."

"Let you out? Sorcha," Adrian said, deciding that they were *definitely* on a first-name basis now, "someone just tried to kill you. Let me help you."

Sorcha bit her lip, looking as if she were internally debating. "Fine," she said, to Adrian's surprise. "Take me to Scotland Yard. But I only want to speak to DCI Stevens. I trust him."

The implication was there. *I don't trust you.* Adrian glanced at Sorcha; her mouth was set in a firm line. There would be no arguing with her.

"OK," Adrian said, though something still seemed... off about Sorcha.

But she shoved the feeling aside. Even if Sorcha only spoke to Stevens, she would finally have some answers.

New Scotland Yard - Art and Antiques Unit
London, England
1:02 P.M.

ADRIAN SAT PERCHED on the edge of the guest desk she shared with Nick, her gaze focused on the closed door of Stevens' office. He and Sorcha had been in there for over half an hour; she had to force herself not to barge in to demand to know what Sorcha was telling him.

"If you're trying to eavesdrop, you're not being very subtle," Nick said, observing her with amusement.

She shot him an annoyed look, but smiled. "Subtlety isn't my strong suit."

He returned her grin. She was relieved that Nick wasn't angry with her after she'd confessed that she'd followed Sorcha. Nick had just told her he wasn't surprised.

"You following Sorcha is a very Adrian West thing to do," he'd said with a shrug.

"What does that mean?"

"You just can't seem to *not* break protocol. It's

something I made myself get used to when we were at the bureau. Irritated the hell out of me, but you did always get results."

"I don't know whether to be offended or flattered," Adrian replied, but she gave him an apologetic smile. "I'm sorry, Nick. We're partners on this; I'm technically just a consultant . . . I should have told you what I was up to."

"Exactly," Nick agreed, giving her a firm look. "Now, that is something the old Adrian would never have done—apologize," he added, returning her smile.

"You didn't catch a glimpse of the shooter?" Nick asked now, following her gaze to Stevens' office.

"No. I think it was a sniper aiming at her from a distance who took off shortly after. If I hadn't been there, he may have taken another shot," Adrian said grimly.

"Who would be shooting at an archaeologist?" Nick asked, raising his eyebrows.

"Especially one with such a flawless background," Adrian echoed, giving him a knowing look.

Before Nick could respond, Stevens' door opened and he stalked toward them. Adrian leapt to her feet, but she stiffened when she saw the stormy look on his face. His usual affable manner was gone; he looked positively furious. He stopped at Nick and Adrian's desk, glowering down at her.

"Why are you harassing Doctor Manning?"

"What?" Adrian gasped.

"Doctor Manning just informed me that you followed her and held her in your car against her will, refusing to let her out until she answered your questions."

Fury coursed through Adrian, and she inwardly cursed herself. Sorcha was still cagey with her after the shooting. She should have known she'd pull something like this. "That's not true. After I rescued her from *shots* being fired at her—"

"Which she wanted to report, but you wouldn't let her until she answered your questions."

"Jack—" Nick intervened, getting to his feet, but Stevens held up his hand, still glowering at Adrian.

"She's not being truthful," Adrian bit out. "Why would I—"

"Do you deny following her?"

"I believe that Doctor Manning is withholding information from this investigation," Adrian said after a brief pause.

"That answers my question," Stevens snapped. "You know, I've heard all about your reputation when you were with the FBI—how difficult you were. But I set aside my misgivings because I thought you could provide valuable insight, especially after the Cleopatra case."

"Jack, come on. There's no need to go there," Nick said tightly.

Adrian clenched her fists at her sides, trying to quell her growing anger. She'd known her reputation from her time with Violent Crimes would never quite go away, but it was still jarring for someone to remind her of it. One of the reasons she had quit law enforcement was to start anew; her academic reputation was now flawless. But then again, the stakes in the world of academia weren't life and death.

"I can't have witness harassment," Stevens said, not backing down. "Adrian, I think it's best if you leave this investigation."

CHAPTER 7

Conwyth Estate
Scottish Highlands
7:06 P.M.

Rage surged through Declan's body as he stalked down the long corridor that led to the main study. A guard hovering by the door stepped forward to stop him, but Declan pushed past him, storming into the study.

Grant was gathered with several other members of the brotherhood, their gazes trained on something on his desk. They stopped talking when he entered.

Declan didn't stop walking until he stood nearly eye to eye with Grant, leveling him with a penetrating glare.

"I told you that Sorcha wasn't going to be a problem. There was no need to try to *kill* her." He nearly shouted the last two words, his jaw clenching.

"I'm afraid there was," Grant returned coolly, waving away the guard who stalked in to take Declan away. "She's been inquiring about the sword. She was even seen getting into the car of an American federal agent."

Ice filled his veins, but he kept his glare locked on Grant's face. "Sorcha won't say anything."

"Are you certain? While she's out there searching for the sword and bringing the police into our orbit, she's a liability." He rose to his full height, returning Declan's glare. "Are you not committed to the cause?"

"I am. You know I am."

"Then you understand that I will do *whatever* is necessary to further it. No one—and I mean no one—will be permitted to get in the way of our ultimate goal."

Declan forced himself to keep his expression neutral, ignoring his conflicting emotions as he gave Grant a curt nod.

"Now," Grant continued, his shoulders relaxing. "Why don't you join us?"

Grant stepped aside, gesturing to his desk. Declan's heart lurched in his chest as his gaze landed on the sword. The hilt had been removed from the sword and dismantled.

"What did you do?" Declan hissed, his rage roaring back to life.

"Calm down," Grant said, holding up his hand. "Look closer."

Declan took a step closer to the desk, leaning in to study the dismantled hilt.

He froze at what he saw. It was faint, but there were *markings* inscribed on the underside of the hilt.

"It appears you were right, my boy," Grant said. "This is one of *the* swords, what the brotherhood has long been searching for. These markings are a message . . . for us."

London, England
7:17 P.M.

ADRIAN STORMED out of Scotland Yard, Nick right behind her, still reeling. She and Nick had tried appealing to Stevens, and though his ire eventually cooled, he insisted it was best that she leave the case. Stevens had even spoken to Briggs about his decision. He didn't want to risk Sorcha filing an official complaint that would go up the chain of command and become a red-tape nightmare.

Nick refused to work without her, so they were now both off the case.

Adrian drew in a breath, anger burning in her gut as she thought of Sorcha's deception. If she thought this would put Adrian off her trail, she was very wrong. This only confirmed that she was hiding something regarding the theft of the artifacts, and whatever it was, it was worth going to these lengths to continue to do so.

"We're not flying back to the US with our tails between our legs," Adrian said, her eyes flashing with determination as they got into her rental car to head back to their hotel.

Nick grinned, but he looked just as determined. "Agreed," he said. "We should—"

He stopped as his phone buzzed, glancing down at it. "It's a text from Vince about the address you sent to him, the one Sorcha went to." He stilled as he read, looking up at her, his face going pale. "It belongs to Maksim Popov, a known weapons dealer."

Adrian's hands tightened on the steering wheel. Why would an archaeologist meet with a weapons dealer? And what did this have to do with an old Iron Age sword?

"Maybe she wants to arrange the sale of the artifacts to weapons dealers," Nick said, reading her mind.

Adrian considered this. While it was possible, it hardly seemed likely.

"How would someone like Sorcha even be connected to a weapons dealer in the first place? And Vince said she comes from money. She hardly needs to sell stolen artifacts," she said.

"Yeah . . . you're right. This proves you were right to follow her," Nick said grudgingly. "And even though we're 'off' the case, who says we can't stay here in London as tourists? You know, as many times as I've been to London, I've never seen Westminster Abbey."

Adrian grinned. When they were partners at the bureau, Nick had always been such a stickler for the rules. But ever since their adventure in Egypt, he'd become increasingly keen to break them.

Nick returned her grin, seeming to read her mind. "You're a bad influence, West."

"Hey, don't blame me," Adrian replied. "This is all you."

As soon as they returned to their hotel, they contacted Briggs from Adrian's room.

"I heard," Briggs said as soon as he answered the video call they placed to him from Adrian's laptop. His expression was tight. "DCI Stevens is not thrilled with you two."

"We got that," Nick said dryly.

Adrian braced herself, waiting for the reprimand, but to her surprise, Briggs said, "I'm assuming the two of you are saying the hell with it and staying on?"

At their mutual look of surprise, Briggs chuckled.

She and Briggs had once been at odds, with Briggs treating her as a murder suspect during her time on the Cleopatra case. She hadn't liked him at first, his superior attitude and by-the-book mentality reminding her of why she'd left the bureau.

Yet ever since she'd solved the Cleopatra case, he'd treated her with nothing but respect, even apologizing for suspecting her. Now, their relationship was professionally amiable, with Nick insisting that Adrian was Briggs' favorite, even though she was no longer an official employee of the FBI. Adrian had to admit that her relationship with Briggs now was better than one she'd ever had with a superior at the bureau.

"Let's be honest. Even if I had ordered you both back to DC, you wouldn't listen to me. And most importantly, Vince told me about the weapons dealer Doctor Manning met with. I think we can all agree there's something more going on here. I'll handle Scotland Yard from here, as much as I can. But be careful and proceed with caution."

CHAPTER 8

Chinnor, England
1:15 P.M.

Briggs provided Adrian and Nick with the location and access code to a safe house located north of London in the village of Chinnor that a CIA contact of his had provided.

The safe house was in fact a nineteenth-century farmhouse with spacious, airy rooms and a quaint garden. It could have easily served as a bed-and-breakfast for tourists visiting the countryside or Londoners wanting a respite from the city. Adrian and Nick had driven here from London after checking out of their hotel that morning.

But Adrian hardly felt like she was on vacation. She leaned against the wall next to the kitchen window that looked out over the garden, nursing the cup of herbal tea she'd made, mentally reviewing the facts of the case. Nick paced back and forth in front of her, his brow furrowed.

"Stolen artifacts—most definitely an inside job, given that the thieves knew the route and which van to target. We were followed by an unknown pursuer on our first day on the case. Sorcha Manning, lead archaeologist on the dig, met with a known weapons dealer—after which she was shot at—then proceeded to lie to Scotland Yard about what happened. But she has a squeaky-clean background."

"We know she's involved somehow," Adrian said. "That's obvious. It's not too much of a stretch to consider that she put that man on us, maybe to make sure we didn't get too close."

"Having worked in Art Crimes, it's not unusual to have museum employees be involved in thefts—in fact, it's common," Nick added. "But Sorcha has been with the British Museum for years. We know she's wealthy, and there's no indication of any type of financial duress in her bank records. She probably doesn't even need that museum job. Plus, she's handled artifacts far more valuable than these . . . the Hereford hoard from a few years ago being one. That was worth hundreds of millions of dollars."

"Exactly," Adrian said. "So why these particular artifacts?" She set down her tea with a frown.

That was the key . . . *these* particular artifacts. She'd have to consider a possibility she'd previously dismissed.

"I can't believe I'm saying this, but Stevens did

mention that the excavators—which had to include Manning—referred to the sword as Excalibur."

Nick raised his eyebrows skeptically.

"I know, I know," she said. "But that sword *is* unique. If Manning believes the sword is linked to the King Arthur myth—"

"Legend," Nick corrected her with a teasing smile.

"—With whatever you want to call it, that has to be what makes this different. Maybe it is as simple as wanting to sell it to that weapons dealer on the black market, even if we don't understand her motive for doing so."

"Then who was shooting at her?" Nick asked. "The thieves she hired to take the sword? Someone who doesn't want her to sell it?"

Adrian expelled a sigh. They were just guessing; they didn't have all the information they needed. In Egypt, during the search for Cleopatra's treasure, they had an expert with them who'd helped them with valuable information they needed to track clues. They needed someone similar . . . someone who could help them fill in the missing pieces.

"If we're looking for the artifacts—mainly, this highly important sword," she said, looking up at Nick, "then we have to find out more about the legend that surrounds it."

"And what's that?"

"Excalibur."

London, England
2:03 P.M.

S̲o̲m̲e̲o̲n̲e̲'s̲ b̲e̲e̲n̲ h̲e̲r̲e̲.

Terror flooded Sorcha's body as she took in her destroyed flat. Someone had completely turned her flat upside down.

The mattress of her king-sized bed was flipped over, all the drawers of her desk and bureau had been emptied, books tossed off their shelves, photo frames smashed; even the living room furniture was upended.

Thankfully, she had nothing here that they might be looking for . . . and she knew exactly who "they" were.

The same people who had tried to kill her.

Sorcha had been careful leaving Scotland Yard after the shooting, taking side streets and blending in with the crowds, her gaze continually scanning her surroundings. She had refused DCI Stevens' offer for a ride back to her flat, or police protection. It was already bad enough that she had spent nearly an hour at Scotland Yard. She'd lied and told him she would contact the police right away if she felt even remotely unsafe.

"Who do you think shot at you?" Stevens had asked.

She'd pleaded ignorance. The theft of the artifacts was high profile, and she was the lead archaeologist on the dig. "I don't know. Perhaps someone thought I had something to do with it. There are a lot of mad people out there."

She hadn't dared tell him the truth.

Sorcha had decided to stay at a hotel under an assumed name for the night and had called in sick to work. Now, as she took in her destroyed flat, she knew that her instincts had been right. It was no longer safe for her in London. She needed to leave, and thanks to a text message she'd received last night while she was at the hotel, along with confirmation from a private investigator that she'd hired ever since the artifacts were stolen, she knew exactly where she was going to go.

Sorcha ran to grab her duffel bag out of the closet and began to hastily toss in some belongings she'd need. She nearly jumped out of her skin when her backup cell phone rang, her body going rigid with fear. She'd ditched her cell phone after leaving Scotland Yard, and only one person had the number of her backup phone, one she'd purchased not long after the artifacts were discovered.

"I heard about the shooting. Are you all right?"

The cultured voice of Michel Laurent filtered through the phone's speaker as she answered, and her shoulders sank with relief.

"Yes. Just shaken. But someone's broken into my flat. I'm leaving London now."

"That's wise. Do you know where you're going to go?"

"Somewhere safe," she lied. If she told him

where she was really going he would do everything in his power to stop her.

"You know what this means? Them trying to kill you?"

"Yes. That I'm on the right track."

"What about the police?"

Sorcha bristled. If he knew about the shooting, of course he knew she'd gone to Scotland Yard. There were strict rules about involving the police.

"I didn't involve them on purpose, Michel. An American agent who's helping them with the case was following me and rescued me from the shooter. But I took care of the police. We should be all right."

"Good. None of them can be trusted."

"I know," Sorcha said. She felt bad for lying to DCI Stevens about West, but ultimately, it was for the pesky American woman's own good. "I've already taken a leave of absence from the museum. Finding the sword is paramount; it's going to be my permanent focus until I get it back. I never should have allowed it to be stolen," she added, guilt making her voice waver.

"You can't blame yourself for that," Michel replied, his tone softening. "Your instructions were clear. If it looked like you had any particular interest in the sword, it would arouse suspicion. You had to treat it just like the other artifacts."

Sorcha knew he was right, but that didn't stop her from feeling responsible for its theft.

Especially when she'd realized who was likely responsible for it.

"You're not alone in this. You never have been. I've been using my resources to track down the sword, and others are looking as well. Why don't you come down to the chateau. We can—"

"That won't be necessary," she said quickly. "Listen, I have to go. I don't want to risk someone else coming here while I'm still in the flat. It's not safe here."

"Of course. But—Sorcha," he said, and there was a long pause before he continued, saying only one word. "Declan."

She stiffened, licking her suddenly dry lips. "What about him?"

"He made his choice."

"I know."

"If he interferes with—"

"I understand."

"Do you?" he pressed.

"Yes," she lied.

"Stay in touch. And Sorcha, stay safe. You know what they are capable of."

CHAPTER 9

Oxford, England
4:32 P.M.

The Bodleian Libraries, situated on the grounds of Oxford University, consisted of research libraries and libraries for various departments of the university. They held over thirteen million items, comprising rare manuscripts and ancient papyri, in addition to art, maps—even music.

The most famous of the libraries was the main Bodleian Library, in continual use since medieval times. One of England's oldest libraries, only the British Library outdid it in size.

As a lover of words and language, Adrian had always loved coming to the Bodleian to take a look at the old manuscripts, and anytime she was in Oxford—or even in London—she would make a point to visit. And as a bonus, with its old Gothic architecture, medieval-domed reading rooms and labyrinth of tunnels that ran underground, visiting the Bodleian was like stepping back in time.

Adrian and Nick were waiting outside of the Bodleian to meet with Finlay Morrow, a professor of medieval classics at Oxford and an Arthurian legend expert. Adrian hoped that Finlay could provide them with some useful information about the legend of Excalibur that could help them with their investigation.

As Finlay approached, Adrian's lips twitched in amusement at Nick's surprised reaction.

Finlay didn't look like the stuffy Oxford type. She was in her late twenties with purple hair, piercings galore, and was by far the hippest historian Adrian knew. She'd met Finlay at an academic conference in London several years prior and had taken an instant liking to her, with her offbeat personality and dry sense of humor. They'd stayed in touch over the years, friending each other on social media, exchanging the occasional email or text, and meeting up whenever they were in each other's neck of the woods.

"I was excited to hear from you," Finlay said, ushering them both inside toward a central courtyard after Adrian introduced her to Nick.

"Thanks for seeing us. I'm sorry this was so last minute," Adrian said, as they took their seats on two long benches in the center of the courtyard.

"You're doing me a favor. I was hoping for an excuse to procrastinate, I've been prepping for a lecture. So you popped in at the right time," Finlay said with a rueful grin. "So. You mentioned in your text that you have some questions for me?"

"We're here in the UK working with Scotland Yard on the Dorset hoard theft," she said, deciding to leave out the fact that they'd just been kicked off the case.

Finlay straightened, her eyes widening in almost comical excitement. "Please don't misunderstand my enthusiasm," she said quickly. "I'm not thrilled about the theft—of course not—I was looking forward to seeing the items for myself once they went up for display. I've just been watching the case with great interest. I'm eager to help in any way I can."

"Among the artifacts, there was a sword of great interest to the excavators. They nicknamed it 'Excalibur' because of the dating and materials the sword was made of. They believe it would have belonged to a 'historical' Arthur," Nick said.

"That's why we're here," Adrian added. "We feel like we're running around in the dark. I was hoping you could fill in some gaps for us about the legendary Excalibur."

"Well, there is a historical basis for the whole pulling a sword out of stone thing," Finlay said. "Back in the day when swords were made, they were removed from stone after being cast in a stone mold. There's also a religious element, in terms of the 'stone' the sword was pulled from. The pagan Britons believed that certain ancient stones represented their gods. There are still such stones standing in Christian churchyards all over modern Britain—Cornwall, Yorkshire, even Wales. As for the 'legendary' Excalibur," Finlay continued, "it came to us from Geoffrey of Monmouth, who of course, gave us much of the Arthurian tale we know today. He called the sword Caliburnus, which was then later translated as Excalibur by medieval French writers. It was initially just described as a very fine weapon, but the supernatural qualities of the sword came later, around the thirteenth century."

Adrian considered what Finlay had told them, but she was still at a loss as to how to link the lore to the here and now. She thought of Sorcha's meeting with the weapons dealer.

"Do you think there could be anything to the sword now? Some way it can be linked to an actual weapon?"

"Well, unless you believe in magic, no," Finlay said, her lips twitching with amusement. "I may be a historian who believes there was a historical Arthur, but even I believe that 'Excalibur' was just a fancy sword that got caught up in some bloody good storytelling."

"Do you know Doctor Sorcha Manning of the British Museum?" Nick asked.

"Of course. She's attended some of my lectures,

and I've consulted on a few exhibits for her department," Finlay said.

"Have you been in contact with her about the missing artifacts?" Adrian asked.

"No, I haven't spoken to her in months." She looked at them in surprise. "You don't think Sorcha has anything to do with the theft, do you?"

Adrian studied her. "What do you think?"

"I may not know her very well, but she comes from family money, so I don't know what her motivations would be," she said. "And the woman is practically a saint. She gives to charity and even makes monthly visits to local hospitals for volunteer work. I think the Queen is more likely to have been behind stealing the artifacts."

"Thanks for your help, Finlay," Adrian said, getting to her feet. "And—due to various circumstances—we'd like to keep our visit here quiet. If anyone asks—"

"You were never here," Finlay said, smiling. "My lips are sealed."

As ADRIAN and Nick headed to where they'd parked their rental, she thought of what Finlay had told them. The best theory she could come up with was that perhaps the thieves believed the sword had an actual link to the "historical" Arthur. But this made Sorcha's involvement even more of a mystery. There was clearly no financial motivation for her to help assist in such a theft.

What was she missing? Were her assumptions wrong?

She turned to Nick, who also looked deep in thought, when she halted in her tracks, spotting a man standing next to their rental car.

He was using a thin strip of metal on one of the windows, trying to break in to it.

Panic flooded her. It was the same man who'd followed them in London.

Adrian darted toward the man. Nick, who'd spotted him as well, was right next to her.

The man immediately took off, turning and dashing into an alley. Adrian and Nick tore after him, determined not to let him get away a second time.

The man raced out of the alley and out onto the other side of the street. Adrian and Nick picked up their pace, trailing him as he abruptly cut into yet another alleyway.

This alleyway, however, did not have an exit, coming to a dead end.

The man whirled to face them, his eyes filled with panic.

Adrian and Nick approached him cautiously. Adrian stepped in front of Nick, knowing he would find her less threatening, holding up her hands to indicate she meant no harm.

"We just want to talk to you," she said.

The man said nothing, his breathing labored.

She could see the wildness in the man's eyes, the sheer panic. He reached into his jacket—

Nick shoved her back, taking out his gun as the man unearthed a knife.

"*Praesidia arma aeternum!*" the man shouted, before reaching up and slicing his own throat.

CHAPTER 10

Oxford, England
10:15 P.M.

Adrian walked brusquely out of the St. Aldates police station, Nick on her heels. She stopped to take a shuddering breath, still shaken from all that had just happened.

Nick had called the local police, who'd taken away the man's body, and they voluntarily went to the police station for questioning. If they'd tried to flee, it would have only made things worse for them, and Adrian didn't want to repeat the experience she'd had in Egypt, being on the run from the authorities. Fortunately, there were street surveillance cameras that had caught the man's suicide on video, so they weren't suspects in his death.

The two local detectives had questioned them extensively. They'd answered honestly, telling them they were here in England on a case and that the man in question had been following them. She knew this would irritate Stevens once word got back to him they were still in the country, but they were safely out of his jurisdiction.

The detectives had identified the man as a James Poole but refused to give them any more information, citing privacy concerns and chain-of-command issues. Before they'd left the station, Nick had reached out to Briggs and Vince to update them, with Vince promising them he'd give them Poole's last known address if he could find it.

They continued on to their rental car. Nick paused, drumming his fingers on the hood as he looked at her.

"Poole's last words," he said. "Do you have any idea what he said?"

"I know he was speaking Latin, but I only made out the word 'praesidia' which means 'protectors,'" Adrian said, chilled as she recalled the wild look in Poole's eyes as he'd uttered the words.

"Great. That can only mean there are more of these wackos out there," Nick muttered.

Adrian nodded, troubled. Poole's death had added yet another question to the many she already had. Why was Poole following them? Who sent him—Sorcha? If so, how did she know where they were?

And what secret did he have that was worth dying for?

Chinnor, England
12:12 A.M.

"Thanks, Vince," Nick said. "Keep me posted."

He hung up, glancing back at Adrian, who sat at the small kitchen table in their safe house. She told him she wanted to jot down what she thought Poole had said, even testing out other languages similar to Latin in case she was wrong about her initial assumption.

Vince had called Nick with updates; it was tricky getting Poole's last known address as he had several aliases that he rented apartments under. Vince did tell him that Poole was born in London to middle-class parents, now deceased, and had a military background, serving two tours in Afghanistan. Poole had spent time in a psychiatric hospital after his time in the military, likely due to lingering PTSD, before essentially disappearing from public record several years ago. No criminal history, nothing.

Nick approached Adrian, updating her with what Vince told him.

"Not to be your parent, but you really should get some sleep. There's not much more we can do until we have an address for Poole," he said.

"You first," Adrian said, looking back down at her work.

"Touché."

She smiled but didn't stop working, jotting down and scratching out words on her notepad, her lovely features tight with concentration. He leaned against the doorway, studying her.

He hadn't realized how much he'd missed her until they were on the Cleopatra case together. They were the perfect counterparts, with her analytical nature paired with risky compulsiveness, and his straightforwardness paired with caution. When Briggs told him he could bring in anyone he wanted on this case, it had already been on the tip of his tongue to ask him if he could bring in Adrian.

"If you're going to stare at me," Adrian grumbled, "you might as well tell me what you're thinking about."

Nick chuckled. "I was thinking . . . I've seen you come back to life, West."

Adrian looked up at him. "What do you mean?"

"You've always been your most passionate when you're on a case. I saw it when we were partners back in the day. I saw it in Egypt, and I'm seeing it now. You should have seen the way your face lit up when I suggested you take on this case with me."

Adrian offered him a smile, but she looked torn. He decided to ask her something that had long been on his mind, even before asking her to join him on this case. "Would you consider staying on? Continuing to work on cases like these in Art

Crimes? I get why you left Violent Crimes, but this is different. I know you can see that."

"I don't know, Nick. I have this whole life that I've built away from the world of criminal investigation," she said, conflict flickering across her face.

Nick took the seat opposite her, holding her gaze. "I never told you this, but about five years ago or so, I was in New York when you gave a guest lecture at Columbia. The one on pre-Columbian writings in the Americas. It was open to the public."

Adrian's eyes went wide with surprise—and hurt. "Why didn't you say hi?"

"It would have been too difficult," he said honestly. "I missed you as a friend, a partner. I probably would have begged you to come back to the bureau, and I do have my pride." He grinned before it faded again, leaning forward. "But there's something I noticed."

"What?"

"Whenever you're discussing a case—whether it's a theory or a way to move forward, it's like a light within you that just turns on. During your lecture, yes, you were excited and somewhat passionate, but it wasn't the same. Not like I've seen how you are now, or even back in Violent Crimes."

Adrian met his gaze, tumult in the depths of her own. He could tell he'd reached her.

"That's just my two cents," he said, holding up

his hands. "And now I'm going to take my own advice and go to bed."

He turned on his heel and headed to his room, thinking of the words he didn't say. How right it felt to have her at his side again. How much he'd miss her if she returned to her old life . . . a life he was certain she no longer belonged in.

CHAPTER 11

Fifty Miles North of London, England
10:17 A.M.

Grief slammed into Sorcha as she veered her car to the shoulder of the busy M40 motorway. She cut the engine and closed her eyes, fighting back the wave of tears that threatened to fall.

"Sorcha?" Michel's concerned voice asked over the phone, which she had on speaker as she drove. "Sorcha?"

"Just—give me a minute," she said, struggling to keep her voice steady, even though she wanted to sob. To scream.

Sorcha had begun her long drive north about an hour ago. She'd left her destroyed flat to stay at another hotel for the night under a different assumed name, wanting to be well rested for her drive to Scotland. In case she was being tracked, she felt safer driving.

Michel had the resources to fly her private, but if he knew where she was going, he would either try to stop her or send in a bunch of his men with her, which would cause a bloodbath. She was just hoping to get to her destination and leave quietly, sword in hand . . . with as little bloodshed as possible

She had just been easing into her long drive when Michel called her, informing her of James Poole's death by his own hand. As her grief washed over her, she wanted to blame West and Harper, but she knew they were blameless. His death was on her hands. She had ordered him to follow them, knowing that he was unstable.

She thought about her friendship with James. He'd shared in her grief over her parents' deaths; he'd been close to them as well. She'd also confided in him about her estrangement with her brother, and her struggles with living up to her family's legacy by serving the brotherhood.

James had in turn told her about the horrors he'd witnessed during his tours of service in Afghanistan, and his efforts to recover from all that he'd seen. They'd shared a genuine bond; he was one of the few friends she had, one who knew all her secrets.

And now he was dead.

Why did you do it, James? she silently screamed. *This wasn't worth your life.*

"We should have never let him join," she said, unable to keep her anguish from her tone. "He was always too—"

"It was what he wanted. He knew the cost."

Michel's voice had lost its softness. He was once again the cold, aristocratic man Sorcha had met years ago when she was still a child, not the father figure he'd eventually become. She knew he was capable of warmth, of caring; he'd been close with her parents and had taken her under his wing after their deaths.

But when it came to the cause, he could become ice cold and determined. He'd never been as close to James as she had been. To him, James was just a resource. A tool to help protect the secret the brotherhood had hidden for centuries.

"Thank you for informing me," she said, forcing the emotion out of her voice. James had given his life to protect the secret; she would do what she must to ensure it wasn't in vain.

"Where exactly are you going?" Michel asked suddenly. "You never did tell me." When she didn't answer right away, his voice rose in urgency. "Sorcha. What are you going to do?"

"What I should have done in the first place," she said, before ending the call, determination rising in her chest as she started her car and pulled back onto the motorway.

∼

Birmingham, England
11:07 A.M.

ADRIAN AND NICK pulled up to a run-down apartment building on the outskirts of Birmingham. Vince had called early that morning with Poole's last known address, and they'd immediately left Chinnor for the nearly two-hour drive north.

"Briggs wanted me to tell you that whatever you choose to do with this information is up to you," Vince had said after Nick put him on speaker. "If you choose to pursue it, we know nothing about it."

Adrian was still tired. She'd slept little; Nick's words the previous night about her academic career had resonated. She hadn't told him she had the same thoughts.

Her academic work had never brought her the same excitement that criminal investigation did. Knowing that she had saved a life or brought a killer to justice gave her a level of satisfaction that delivering a solid lecture or publishing a well-researched paper simply didn't. She kept reminding herself of the reasons she'd left the bureau in the first place. The red tape, the constant battles with her superiors, the interdepartmental conflicts. That last, awful case before she'd finally quit.

But she still felt . . . uncertain.

Adrian forced aside her tumultuous thoughts; she needed to focus only on this case for now.

She exchanged a glance with Nick before getting out and approaching the apartment building. They both knew what they were about to do was dangerous and, frankly, illegal. But they didn't have the time to go through all the international wrangling it would take to get a warrant to search Poole's apartment. They needed information, and they needed it fast.

The building, unsurprisingly, had no secured entrance. They were able to enter with ease, making their way up to the third floor. The air was heavy with the stench of mold, and the old wooden floor creaked dangerously beneath their feet. They moved carefully; Poole's apartment was at the far end of the corridor.

Adrian stood aside as Nick easily picked the flimsy lock and swung open the door.

Poole's apartment was a small studio that looked barely lived in. The only furniture was a thin mattress on the floor and a chair. Adrian moved over to the mattress, lifting it to see if there was anything hidden beneath. To her surprise, there were two visibly loose floorboards. She lifted them, seeing that they led to a crawlspace large enough to fit a man, possibly two. But it was empty.

Disappointed, she turned her attention to a small duffel bag that was perched on the chair. She searched through it while Nick looked through the cabinets above the miniscule stove.

The bag was just full of old clothes. She nearly set it aside, but spotted a bronze pendant at the bottom. Pushing the clothes aside, she retrieved it from the bag.

"Nick. Take a look at this."

Nick came over and knelt next to her as she held up the pendant, flipping it open.

Inside, there were letters inscribed on the center in a circular pattern, in no discernible order.

"It must be a hidden message or code," she said, looking up at Nick.

"Of course it is," Nick said with a sigh. "Any way of decoding it?"

"After all my brainstorming last night, I concluded that his last words were in fact Latin," she said, "so I'm going to assume that if there's a message hidden here, it's in Latin. It could possibly be a cryptogram. Since this is engraved, it's probably an older type of code . . . something like a classical cypher. That's how I'll try to decrypt it."

Adrian knew she was making a lot of assumptions, but at the moment, she had nothing else to go on. She took out her phone and transcribed the letters into a document application on her phone.

"So how does this work?" Nick asked. "Don't you need a key to decrypt a cryptogram?"

Adrian didn't answer right away, studying the letters on her phone. She knew how to read classical Latin, so she hoped she was right about her assumption that if there was a hidden code, it was in Latin.

"Yep. But when you don't have one, you can use something called frequency analysis," she said.

She glanced up from her phone, giving him an admonishing look. "Didn't you take the cryptography course at the academy?"

"That was optional. I'm not a nerd, West."

"Says the art history major," she wryly returned, turning her focus back to the letters.

"That was purely because I had a crush on a girl who was majoring in it," Nick said, shrugging. "I didn't learn a thing."

"Well, if you had taken the cryptography class, you would know that frequency analysis works by identifying how often certain letters in the cipher appear, then using some guesswork to link related letters to them."

"OK," Nick said slowly.

"In Latin, the most common letters are I, E, and A. So, we can assume that—"

"Many of the letters on the pendant correspond to each of those letters."

"Exactly. I'll start with I," Adrian said, chewing on her bottom lip as she carefully decoded several of the letters on the pendant.

Nick fell silent, allowing Adrian to concentrate, as she carefully replaced the letters until she had a workable key.

"OK," she said, when she was finished. "Now I'm going to use the words I substituted. It won't be a perfect match, but it may get me close."

She carefully transcribed the letters using the key she'd come up with. Nick moved to look down at her phone as she typed out the letters, but they didn't form anything decipherable.

"Doesn't make much sense," Nick supplied, helpfully.

"My key must be wrong," she said, gritting her teeth with frustration. "On to the next letter. You work on E. I'll work on A."

As Adrian and Nick got to work transcribing, the sudden sound of footsteps thundering down the corridor made her freeze. Nick went still as well, his hand going to his weapon.

The footsteps were coming right toward them.

CHAPTER 12

11:17 A.M.

Adrian held her breath, her heart slamming violently against her rib cage.

The floorboards above her rattled as the heavy boots of several men moved around the small apartment.

Adrian and Nick were curled up in the crawlspace they'd found beneath the mattress. Nick had managed to partially drag the mattress over the floorboards they were lying beneath just before the door to Poole's apartment had crashed open. They'd had no time to escape; it was the best option they had in the moment.

She and Nick were pressed tightly together; she could feel his thundering heartbeat. Despite the danger of the moment, a fissure of arousal wound its way through her, as well as comfort at being so close to him. Adrian ignored the persistent pull of desire, leaning in to the feeling of comfort instead. She and Nick had faced many dangerous moments before, and despite being more than capable of holding her own, she always felt safer with him at her side.

Together, they listened to the heavy footsteps of the men above. The men spoke little, but the few words she did hear were British English. It sounded like one man was ordering the other two around. Mercenaries? Soldiers? How were they linked to James Poole?

Her heart nearly stopped as she heard a pair of footsteps stop right above where she and Nick were hiding.

"Richard, you finding anything?"

"Not a bloody thing," the third man replied. "But from what I was told, the man lived like a monk."

There were more footsteps and shuffling around, until finally, the leader said, "It's no use. There's nothing here."

Relief washed over Adrian as she heard the men make their way to the door. Her relief was short-lived as one set of footsteps paused by the door. In her mind's eye, she could practically see the man's gaze sweeping over the small apartment.

Her chest tightened as his footsteps came back into the apartment once more, the steps slow and deliberate. Her pulse raced as the steps stopped right by the mattress that hid their crawlspace.

She could hear him kick the mattress aside. Could feel his gaze boring into the floor.

The seconds seemed to drag on for an eternity until she heard one of the other men call out from the corridor, telling him he had a call. The man seemed to linger above them for several long moments before his footsteps finally retreated out of the apartment, closing the door behind him.

Adrian and Nick remained still for some time until Nick cautiously pushed back the floorboards. He crawled out, Adrian following suit.

She immediately made her way to the window that overlooked the street. There was no sign of the men.

They didn't wait a second longer, slipping out of the apartment, exiting through a back entrance that led out to a dingy alleyway, scanning their surroundings as they headed back to their rental car.

"Who do you think they were?" Nick asked as soon as they were in their car, heading out of the city.

"They sounded like hired help. Mercenaries. No doubt linked to the stolen artifacts."

She took the pendant out of her pocket, determination rising as she looked down at it. If she could decode it, she had the feeling it would give them some kind of answer.

As Nick drove, taking side roads and frequently checking the rearview mirror in case they were being followed, she tried to solve the cryptogram using the letter A, but it only rendered more gibberish. She tried again, this time using the letter E.

Adrian stilled as she typed out an actual discernible message.

"Nick."

Nick glanced over as Adrian held up her phone. The decoded message read—

PRAESIDIA ARMA
SEDIS GENTIS DEARGAN

"*Praesidia arma,*" Adrian said, lowering her phone to look down at the screen. "That's Latin for 'protectors of the weapon.' That must be what James Poole said before he killed himself. 'Sedis Gentis Deargain' means 'Seat of Clan Deargain.'"

She met Nick's eyes, her heart hammering. "The message refers to a place."

CHAPTER 13

Conwyth Estate
Scottish Highlands
1:07 P.M.

Declan hovered next to Grant, who glowered down at the petite woman with purple hair named Finlay.

They were all gathered in the study; Grant had summoned him here shortly after Finlay arrived. There was still tension between him and Grant; he was still infuriated that Grant had sent someone after Sorcha. Declan had secretly contacted Sorcha for the first time in years the previous evening, sending her a warning via text message to stop looking for the sword, to leave the country for her own safety, ignoring the texts she'd sent in reply. He told his troubled conscience that he had at least done something to protect her from Grant.

You could do more, a phantom voice whispered,

which he forced himself to ignore. He'd dedicated himself to the cause; he wouldn't back down now.

He couldn't.

Now, he studied Finlay, finding it hard to believe that this pixie was a member of the brotherhood, even though Grant had told him her late parents had been members, and she was firmly dedicated to the brotherhood's mission.

"Miss Morrow here just informed us that she had a lovely chat with two American federal agents searching for the sword," Grant said, his fists clenched at his sides.

Declan stiffened with surprise and suspicion, but Finlay held her own, glaring right back at Grant. In fact, She didn't look at all intimidated by Grant or Declan.

"One of those agents—a *former* agent, I might add—is Adrian West. I know her. If I had withheld anything, she would have suspected me. That woman can sniff out deceit a mile away. I could tell she nor her partner knew anything. Their focus was on Sorcha Manning." She let out a snort of disbelief. "I think they believe she's behind the theft of the artifacts. I told them generic historical facts about the legend of Excalibur. I even attested to Sorcha's innocence to throw them off the scent."

Declan's body went rigid at the mention of Sorcha, but he kept his expression neutral.

"And James Poole?" Grant pressed.

"I didn't know that nutcase was following them," Finlay snapped. "Now. If you're done questioning me, do you want my help with the sword or not? I assume that's why you sent for me?"

After several long moments, Grant gave her an abrupt nod. Finlay moved past him to the desk, where the dismantled sword rested.

Finlay's eyes widened in awe, and Declan felt a wave of appreciation. Many of the mercenaries Grant had hired took the significance of the sword for granted. He could tell that Finlay admired it as much as he did.

She put on a pair of gloves that Grant handed her as she lifted the hilt of the sword, running her fingers over the markings inscribed there.

"The Ogham script," she whispered. "Of course they would use the Ogham script."

"Our experts have already determined that," Grant said dismissively. "But so far they haven't been able to understand what the letters they've decoded could mean. They're not certain the language—it could be Latin, primitive Irish, even Pictish."

"Give me some time," Finlay said, rifling around in her bag.

"Don't take too long," Grant said. "Time is of the essence."

Finlay shot him an annoyed look. "I'm aware of the stakes, Grant."

Grant's face reddened, but Finlay ignored him, focused entirely on the sword. Again, Declan was impressed by Finlay's lack of intimidation around Grant, something which clearly irritated the older man. She was treating Grant Macleod, the wealthy and influential leader of the brotherhood, as if he were a nuisance.

"Fine. You know where your room is," Grant said tightly. "I'll check on you in a couple of hours. Declan will stay with you."

"I don't need one of your goons looking over me," Finlay snapped.

"Declan. Will. Stay. With. You," Grant returned, giving Declan a firm look before leaving the room.

Finlay waited until Grant left the room, rolling her eyes. "That man has a giant stick up his arse," she announced, turning her attention back to the inscriptions.

Declan had to stifle a laugh, trying to force a stern expression on his face. Finlay lifted the digital microscope she'd unearthed from her bag, zooming in on the inscriptions.

"It's a shame Sorcha picked the wrong side," she said idly.

Declan couldn't help bristling at the words, tamping down the instinct to defend Sorcha. He knew Grant had cameras in the room and would likely be watching them. Grant barely trusted him as it was, it would do no good to defend Sorcha.

"What made you join Grant's side?" Finlay continued.

Declan was tempted not to answer. There was something in her tone he didn't like. Despite his earlier admiration of how she'd stood up to Grant, she was starting to irritate him.

"Keeping the weapon hidden is a mistake," he said finally. "The ancient brotherhood was wrong to do so. Once we find it, we'll make certain it doesn't fall into the wrong hands."

Finlay looked up from the sword, her eyes wide with disbelief.

"Is that what Grant told you?" she asked in a low voice.

Unease prickled along the base of his spine. *Don't listen to her*, he told himself. *She's just trying to sow doubt.*

But he already had doubts. They'd started as soon as he saw an innocent young driver shot before his eyes.

"I'll not say any more, because I know the paranoid bastard has cameras in the room," Finlay said, keeping her voice low. "But you should find out what Grant *really* plans to do with the weapon when he finds it."

CHAPTER 14

Airspace over Derbyshire, England
5:37 P.M.

Adrian looked out over the clouds as the plane she and Nick were on flew north, hoping they were on the right track.

It had taken some research, but they'd determined where the words on the pendant led to. An estate nestled in the Scottish Highlands, roughly forty miles south of Inverness. The estate had originally been built by the chieftain of the Deargain clan, the name on Poole's pendant. The estate currently belonged to a private owner. As soon as they'd learned its location, they'd booked the next flight out from Birmingham to Inverness.

They had debated whether to tell Briggs where they were going. Adrian was wary of telling him, fearful he'd insist they not go without backup, which would take time to arrange. But Nick had insisted it was best to keep Briggs in the loop. If they were going to the right place, they would need backup, and Briggs would have a line to the local authorities to help them with that.

He'd ultimately convinced her, and they'd spoken to Briggs before leaving. Briggs had indeed told them not to approach or enter the estate, but to survey it from a distance and report back while Vince performed a thorough check into whoever currently lived there. That was another benefit to keeping Briggs and Vince in the loop, she had to grudgingly admit. Vince could get information they had difficulty accessing on their own.

The flight they were on was thankfully brief. As soon as they arrived at Inverness Airport, they rented a car and made their way south toward the Highlands.

Adrian took in the sweeping vistas around them. The sky was awash with an array of colors, from purple to pink to orange as the sun set beyond the horizon. Rolling green hills and mountains in the distance surrounded them, punctuated in between by sprawling glens that glittered beneath the fading sun. The Scottish Highlands, relatively isolated for a large swath of his history, had once been home to battling clans who dominated these lands, lands they knew well, for centuries. Even now it felt distant and isolated from the other bustling cities of the UK, and she increasingly realized how alone she and Nick were . . . and what a risk they were taking.

"Briggs is right. When we get there, we should hang back at a distance," she said. "See if there are any men patrolling the grounds. We need to know what we're up against if we need backup."

"Got it," Nick agreed. "And no Adrian West impulsiveness, OK? If there's an army of those mercenaries we saw back at Poole's apartment . . ."

"Me, impulsive?" Adrian asked, holding up her hands in mock innocence. "I don't know what you mean."

Roughly half an hour later, just after the sun had taken its final descent, they turned onto a narrow road that led to a sprawling estate in the distance.

Nick pulled over and killed the lights; they both pulled out binoculars they'd picked up in Birmingham before catching their flight north.

Adrian peered through her binoculars, her heart sinking, because she could vaguely make out men patrolling the grounds . . . and they were armed. She lowered her binoculars, defeat settling over her. She shouldn't have been surprised; whoever was involved in this whole thing had to have resources to keep the estate under careful guard. This was the complete opposite of breaking into a shitty studio apartment. There was no way they could get near the place without backup. They had no choice but to call Briggs.

"I see you're thinking what I'm thinking," Nick said with a sigh. "I'm going to call Briggs—see if we can get backup. It may take a few hours to deal with all the hoops he has to jump through, but the local FBI office can help. Answers have to be in that estate."

Adrian nodded her agreement. As much as she hated to alert whoever was in the estate to their presence, she knew it was their best bet for getting inside.

Just as Nick took out his phone, an SUV suddenly sped toward them from behind, screeching to a halt right next to them. Another car pulled up in front of them, caging them in.

Panic tore through Adrian as several armed men emerged from the SUV and approached, aiming rifles at them.

An intimidatingly large man stepped forward, his dark eyes glittering with danger.

"You're coming with us or we start shooting."

CHAPTER 15

Conwyth Estate
Scottish Highlands
8:02 P.M.

The burly man who'd grabbed Nick was *not* gentle. Nick could already feel a bruise forming on his upper arm from the man's rough handling.

After Adrian and Nick had stepped out of the car, he'd tried to step in front of Adrian, but his tough partner had already whirled on the men, lowering her body to kick out at one of them. The strike landed between one man's thighs and he'd let out a pained groan.

Another man had lurched forward to grab Adrian and restrain her. Fury had raced through him, and Nick managed to twist out of the grip of the man holding him to race toward his partner, but another man punched him in the gut.

One of the men then blindfolded Nick and put him into a car. The men ignored his pleas to free Adrian during the short drive, after which they roughly removed Nick from the car and led him inside what he assumed was the estate.

Nick nearly stumbled when he was shoved forward onto the descending stairs, and he heard the man behind him let out a chuckle. *Asshole.* The man forced Nick the rest of the way down the stairs and a long corridor before he was pushed into another room that smelled musky and damp. *Basement? Cellar?*

His handlers shoved him into a chair, binding his hands and legs. The blindfold was then snatched off his face.

The same tall, dark-haired man who'd ordered them from the car glared down at him.

"Who are you?" he demanded.

"Where is my partner?" Nick returned. "I'm not answering any questions until I know she's safe."

His new best friend, the burly man who stood at Nick's side, punched him in the gut at his response. Nick keeled over, gritting his teeth to stop himself from crying out in pain.

"You are in no position to be making demands," the man hissed. "I will ask you one last time. Who are you, and why are you here?"

Nick remained stubbornly silent, glaring at him. The man expelled a sigh.

"Very well," he said, taking a menacing step forward.

Nick closed his eyes, bracing himself for the pain.

The ropes binding Adrian's arms and legs to the chair dug painfully into her flesh, but she ignored the discomfort, glaring at the older, refined man who sat in front of her.

She was in a spacious and ornate study. The man sat perched on the edge of his desk, arms folded, a pleasant smile on his face, as if they were merely sharing a cup of tea. Another man, a guard, stood several feet to her left, his hand lightly resting on the gun holstered at his hip.

"I don't want to hurt you, love. I consider myself a gentleman and would never lay hands on a woman. Especially not one as lovely as yourself. However," his voiced lowered, taking on a dangerous edge, "I will do what I must."

Adrian didn't react, keeping her gaze steady on his.

"Now tell me," the man said, the pleasant smile returning to his face. "Who are you, and why are you here?"

Adrian didn't respond. The man didn't look surprised by her lack of response. He merely shrugged and rose to his feet.

"OK," he said, rolling up his shirt sleeves. Adrian braced herself, and the man noticed, giving her a dark smile. "I just said I won't harm a woman. I will if I have to. I just want to reacquaint you with someone first." He turned to the door, raising his voice. "Bring her in.

To Adrian's astonishment, a guard dragged in an angry and struggling Finlay. At first Adrian feared he had also taken Finlay hostage, but she shook free of the guard and glared at the man.

"Grant, what the hell is this?" Finlay hissed.

"Did your friend Finlay tell you about us?" Grant asked Adrian, ignoring Finlay.

"Finlay?" Adrian gasped, but Finlay didn't spare her a glance.

"Are you serious? You still don't trust me?" Finlay snapped. "I told you how West is—she was bound to find this place. Kill her and be done with it."

Disbelief coursed through Adrian. She was behaving nothing like the friendly, warm Finlay that Adrian knew. Grant was watching Adrian closely, clearly checking for any subterfuge.

"If you need my help, you'll let me get back to my work," Finlay said, still glowering at Grant.

Grant studied Finlay and then Adrian's astonished face for another beat before letting out a low chuckle. "My apologies, Miss Morrow," he said. "I won't bother you again."

As Finlay stalked past her, looking more annoyed than anything else, Adrian couldn't help herself.

"Finlay," she whispered. "Why?"

Finlay didn't respond. She merely gave her a cold, dismissive glance before leaving the study.

When the door shut behind her, Adrian closed her eyes, chilled to the bone.

"It seems you didn't truly know your friend Finlay," Grant said, shaking his head. "She's one of us, as were her parents."

Adrian pushed past her shock, turning her focus to Grant. "Who is . . . us?"

"You answer my question first, Miss West," Grant replied. When she remained silent, he heaved a sigh. He reached over and picked up an iPad that had been resting on his desk, pressing a button before holding it up for her to see.

Terror flooded Adrian's body at the video streaming on the screen. Nick was seated in a cellar, slumped over and eerily still, his face badly bruised and bleeding. The terror faded, and white-hot fury shot through her; she jerked forward in her chair.

Grant smiled, as if amused by her reaction. "Now, your partner, I have no problem with hurting. And I'll keep hurting him until he's dead. Unless you start talking."

Adrian remained frozen, her heart in her throat. Grant let out another sigh before picking up his phone, still holding up the iPad. The large man in the room with Nick answered the phone.

"Wolfe, you have my permission to—" Grant began.

"Wait," she said. She knew what Nick would want her to do. *Chill out, West. I can take a beating.*

But *she* couldn't allow him to take a beating. She would tell this man enough of the truth to keep him satisfied, and perhaps play upon some of his "gentlemanly" airs. Briggs knew that she and Nick were here; she just needed to buy some time.

"Never mind," Grant said, "but be on standby."

Grant raised his eyebrows as he studied her, lowering the iPad.

"I'll tell you who we are and why we're here," she said, "but first, can you at least loosen my binds? They're hurting me."

"No," Grant said immediately. "I may be a gentleman, but I'm not a fool. I can tell you have some power in that lovely frame of yours. One of my men is still recovering from your attack on his . . . nether regions." He chuckled with amusement before his expression turned dark again. "Now. Who are you?"

"I'm a professor from New York University in the States," she said, telling him information she was certain he already knew. Finlay had mentioned her by name, so he clearly knew who she was. "I'm also a former federal agent. I came to England to consult with the Scotland Yard Art and Antiques Unit on the theft of the stolen artifacts from Dorset."

"And your boyfriend?"

"He's a current federal agent."

"And why are you two here, Miss West? Or rather, how did you know to come here?"

"Let Nick go first and I'll tell you everything."

Grant frowned, but he did look as if he was considering her request. As Adrian studied him, she saw something out of the corner of her eye.

It was a woman who passed by the open door of the study so quickly she almost looked like an apparition. Yet Adrian had seen her, and she swore the woman pressed a finger to her lips.

Though she only got a brief glimpse of the woman, she recognized her.

The woman was Sorcha Manning.

Sorcha kept telling herself that she'd just come here for the sword.

She'd never wanted to set foot in this place again; there were too many painful memories. But she knew ultimately there was nowhere else the sword could be.

Sorcha had known in her gut that Grant was behind the theft, but she wasn't certain of his location. She hadn't thought that he would hide in plain sight, in the estate she'd spent part of her childhood in. The private investigator she'd hired had confirmed his location. That information, along with Declan's text to her last night, had all but confirmed that the sword was here.

She could only pray she didn't run into Declan.

If she did, she didn't know if she could stop herself from killing him, or breaking down and begging him to come with her. Even though it was years ago, his betrayal still weighed on her.

She'd arrived at the estate not long after they'd taken those two pesky American agents inside. Sorcha herself had made a pit stop in nearby Inverness to pick up a weapon—a pistol with a silencer—from a trusted contact. West and Harper distracting the guards had allowed Sorcha to sneak in through a side entrance. Fortunately for her, the old codes that opened the gates hadn't been changed in years. Her intent was to get the sword and flee. Adrian West and Nick Harper were not her responsibility; she'd done all she could to get them thrown off the case. She didn't know why they were still sniffing around.

Sorcha told herself this would be an even easier way for her to get the sword. If the guards were all focused on Adrian and Nick, then it was possible for her to get the sword and leave unimpeded.

But her pesky conscience kept bothering her. These men were murderers, with their leader being the deadliest of them all. Adrian and Nick wouldn't make it out alive. Two voices warred inside her—one that told her it wasn't her problem, another that told her she couldn't allow them to die.

The latter voice eventually won out. She already had James' death on her conscience. And wasn't she involved in all of this to prevent mass death and suffering? Besides, Adrian had rescued her from bullets on the streets of London. She owed her one.

She made her presence known by slipping past the open door of the study and pressing her finger to her lips. Adrian's eyes briefly locked with hers, but the woman had one hell of a poker face, because she didn't react.

Sorcha knew this estate like the back of her hand. She used this knowledge to her advantage to slip down side halls and corridors, out of sight of the few patrolling guards she spotted.

She eventually found the circuit breaker, located at the base of a set of winding stairs that led to one of the cellars.

Sorcha took a deep breath. *Here goes nothing.*

She reached out to kill the lights, plunging the entire estate into darkness.

CHAPTER 16

8:27 P.M.

"Tell me how you found our estate. I'm starting to lose my patience," Grant snarled.

Adrian kept her expression neutral, though her pulse was racing.

What was Sorcha doing here? She tried not to let herself hope, but if Sorcha were with these men, she wouldn't have snuck by and indicated for Adrian to keep quiet.

Adrian needed to keep buying time.

"We were looking at old estates in the Highlands, hoping that—"

"THE TRUTH!" Grant roared.

All of his gentlemanly composure had slipped, his face contorted with fury. He stepped toward her, raising his fist to strike, but the study was plunged into sudden darkness. She could hear the panicked shouts of the guards echoing around the estate.

Adrian sprang into action. Still attached to her chair, she got to her feet and reared back to smash it against the wall. Once, twice, until a leg broke off.

In the darkness, she could make out both the guard and Grant lunging toward her. Using all the strength she possessed, she yanked her hand free of one of the bonds tying her to the chair, reaching down to grab the broken chair leg. Just as Grant and the guard reached her, she struck them both as hard as she could—Grant across the temple, the guard in the crotch. Grant slumped to the floor, while the guard went to his knees with a snarl of pain.

Adrian raced out of the study, nearly colliding with another figure as she exited. Expecting it to be another guard, she raised the chair leg, prepared to strike—

But it was Sorcha.

Sorcha shoved Adrian out of the way, raising her hand, which held a pistol. She fired a silenced shot out at the guard who charged after Adrian. He slumped to the floor.

Sorcha gestured for Adrian to turn around, which she did, and quickly undid her binds, releasing her from the chair.

"We don't have much time," Sorcha said. "They have your partner in the cellar. I know of a way out."

Adrian followed Sorcha as she crept back down

the corridor away from the study, using a flashlight to guide their way, though she had a million questions. What was Sorcha's connection to this place? Why was she here? With the way she'd effortlessly shot the guard, it wasn't her first time using a gun.

But now was not the time to ponder any of this. She just needed to get to Nick and get the hell out of here.

Adrian trailed Sorcha down the corridor until they reached a set of stairs that led to a lower level. They moved cautiously until they reached the lower level. As soon as they reached it, two guards raced toward them from the opposite end of the corridor.

Sorcha immediately fired, sending both guards slumping to the ground. Sorcha and Adrian broke into a run as the footsteps of more guards approaching from above sounded.

"This way!" Sorcha shouted, taking a sharp left from the main corridor, which led to another set of stairs. Adrian raced down the stairs after Sorcha, where they made their way down yet another narrow corridor.

As they approached a cellar door at the end of it, Adrian could hear grunts and groans inside, fists slapping flesh. Panic clogged Adrian's throat. Was Nick successfully fighting back or losing the battle?

Sorcha approached the door and entered a code on a keypad right outside of it, holding up her pistol as she and Adrian entered.

Nick was fighting a losing battle against a

guard; he had Nick on the ground and was pummeling him in the face.

Fury shot through Adrian and she stepped forward, but Sorcha stopped her, expertly firing a shot at the guard who crumpled as Nick rolled out from under him.

Adrian rushed forward, helping Nick to a sitting position. She touched his bruised face. "Are you all right?"

"It looks worse than it feels," he said, though he grimaced when she touched his face.

"We have to hurry—I know a way out," Sorcha said from behind them.

Nick gave Sorcha a puzzled look, but Adrian just shook her head. There was no time for explanations now.

They hurried after Sorcha, who sprinted farther down the corridor. To her surprise, Sorcha approached the wall, pushing on it and revealing a separate tunnel.

"Come on!" she shouted.

Adrian and Nick entered; Sorcha slid the wall shut behind them. Using her flashlight to illuminate their surroundings, Sorcha moved forward with Adrian and Nick on her tail. The tunnel was narrower than the corridor they'd come from and almost pitch black. Adrian didn't know how long they walked until they reached a set of rickety stairs that led up to a small, circular opening.

Just as they approached the stairs, a man's voice rang out.

"Sorcha."

They whirled. A tall, dark-haired man who bore a resemblance to Sorcha stood a dozen feet behind them. He had a pistol, but it was lowered to his side, his focus trained on Sorcha.

"Declan," Sorcha breathed, lowering her weapon.

"Go," Declan said sharply. "The others will be here soon."

Sorcha stiffened with surprise, hope flaring in her eyes. "Dec . . . you're my brother, and I still love you. I don't care what's happened in the past. Come with us."

Adrian stiffened at the sound of approaching guards, coming from the far end of the tunnel.

"I can't," he said. "But you need to go. Now."

"Declan—"

"GO!" he roared, firing his gun into the air.

Sorcha remained rooted to the spot, her body trembling with emotion.

Adrian lurched forward, gripping Sorcha's hand. She feared Sorcha would fight her, that she and Nick would have to physically drag her out, but Sorcha allowed Adrian to lead her up the stairs and into the waiting night.

CHAPTER 17

Fifteen Miles West of Alford, Scotland
9:34 P.M.

"I know you have many questions," Sorcha said, when they were a safe distance away from the estate, her car barreling down the A95 motorway. "And I'll answer them once we get to a safe place. There's an apartment in Aberdeen I have access to that the brotherhood doesn't know about."

When they'd emerged from the tunnel, Sorcha had led them to her car, which was tucked away in a nearby cluster of trees. They'd used the cover of darkness to escape; Adrian suspected that Declan must have distracted or misdirected their pursuers, because no one immediately came after them. Sorcha had taken small side roads until reaching the main motorway leading east.

"The brotherhood?" Adrian echoed, thinking

of the words James Poole had uttered, and the words on the pendant. *Praesidia arma*.

"Like I said," Sorcha repeated, her gaze remaining on the road, "I'll answer your questions once we're in Aberdeen."

Adrian heeded Sorcha's words and fell silent as she drove, though she was practically bursting with questions. She now knew why Sorcha was so cagey about answering their questions back in London. Her own brother was involved in the theft, something she seemed to be aware of. Yet by their interaction, it seemed they were estranged.

Sorcha also knew the estate intimately; she'd managed to sneak onto it and knew where everything was, including the hidden tunnel that led to their escape. Did Sorcha know Grant, their captor?

And Adrian wanted to know exactly what Sorcha knew about the sword. Why was it so important?

Adrian's thoughts turned to Finlay, who was also connected to all of this. She was an excellent actress, because Adrian hadn't gotten a hint of anything untoward when she and Nick had questioned her at the Bodleian. A chill swept over her at the casual way Finlay had disregarded her life, how she'd looked at Adrian as if she were nothing. She and Finlay were hardly best friends, but Finlay had always treated Adrian with kindness. As a former criminal profiler, Adrian was usually excellent at reading people. How could she have been so wrong about Finlay?

Adrian kept her tumultuous thoughts to herself during the remainder of the drive, keeping silent until they arrived in the port city of Aberdeen, periodically scanning the surrounding streets to make certain they weren't being followed. She could see that Nick was doing the same in the back seat.

Sorcha took them to an apartment not far from the University of Aberdeen that belonged to a professor friend of hers who was currently out of the country, located in the neighborhood of Aberdeen aptly named Old Aberdeen.

Old Aberdeen was first settled by scholars and traders alike during medieval times, and it was now a quaint district consisting of winding cobblestoned streets and dotted with towering medieval buildings, including Saint Machar's Cathedral, built in the fourteenth century, and the old—and modern—buildings of the University of Aberdeen.

When they entered the spacious two-bedroom apartment, Adrian and Nick thoroughly checked the entire apartment out of habit, though Sorcha insisted it was safe.

Adrian made Nick sit on the bulky couch in the small living room as Sorcha brought out first-aid materials from the bathroom to take care of Nick's facial wounds. He again insisted he was fine as Adrian cleaned and dressed his wounds, anger filling her at what he must have gone through at the hands of those men.

Sorcha then brought them tea and sandwiches

from the kitchen. Adrian set down her tea, leaning forward, eager to finally get some answers.

"First of all, thank you," Adrian said. "You no doubt saved our lives."

"I owed you one," Sorcha said. "Now we're even."

"I also think we're owed an explanation for all this. Your words to DCI Stevens got us kicked off the case," Adrian continued, trying to keep her voice even, though remnant anger threatened to bubble to the surface.

"I'm sorry about that, I really am. But it was for your own good," Sorcha insisted. "We—I'm handling the stolen artifacts. It's best to not get anyone else involved."

"You do realize we're law enforcement, right?" Nick asked her in disbelief. "If anyone is going to get involved, it would be us."

"This is far more dangerous than either of you understand," Sorcha said.

"Enough with the cryptic comments," Adrian said, impatient. "Let's get to the point. You know who took the artifacts and the sword. And why were you meeting with a known arms dealer the day I rescued you from being shot back in London?"

"I was getting information about the artifacts. A contact of mine told me he'd been in touch with Grant Macleod, who I suspected was behind the theft. Maksim Popov has a thing for redheads," she said, looking mildly disgusted. "I was hoping he would be amenable and tell me Grant's whereabouts, or if he knew anything about the artifacts. But all he did was make passes at me."

"You chose to show up to Grant's estate without telling the authorities. Is it just because your brother was involved? Or some other reason?" Adrian pressed.

"It's—complicated," Sorcha hedged.

"*Answers*, Sorcha. Or we will have no choice but to get all types of authorities involved, something you clearly don't want. We're obviously on the same side. Let us help you."

Sorcha stared at them for several moments and then lowered her gaze, as if debating with herself. Finally, she expelled a breath.

"I didn't want to say anything because I know the people involved. We used to all be a part of the same organization."

"The same organization?" Nick pressed.

"Yes. It's officially called 'Praesidia Arma'. We just call it the brotherhood, which it's been unofficially known as for centuries."

Adrian leaned forward. "And what is the point of this brotherhood?"

"To protect a secret."

"What kind of secret?" Nick asked. "Excalibur?"

"Yes, and no. But it's not what you're thinking," Sorcha said, shaking her head. "This isn't about that King Arthur fairy-tale Excalibur nonsense."

"Then tell us what it is about," Adrian pressed.

"Well, for one thing, there was never an Arthur, or an Excalibur—at least, not in the way most people think. Excalibur isn't a weapon. It never was." She hesitated before continuing. "It's a place."

CHAPTER 18

Fifty Miles South of Inverness, Scotland
10:37 P.M.

Grant pressed the barrel of his pistol tightly into the flesh beneath Declan's chin, but Declan held still, meeting his infuriated eyes.

They were in Grant's private car on the way to Inverness Airport. Grant had ordered everyone to leave the estate grounds after Sorcha and the others escaped; he believed the police's arrival would be imminent.

In the moments after Sorcha and the Americans had fled, several of Grant's men had entered the tunnel from which they'd escaped. Declan had pretended to be wounded, telling them they had gotten the drop on him and fled. They'd seemed to take him at his word, though he noticed that a couple of them looked at him with suspicion.

Grant had said nothing to Declan besides ordering him to accompany him in his private car to the airport; he was flying to his home in Edinburgh along with the sword, Finlay, and a couple of other experts were in a separate car. Once they were on the road, Grant had ordered the driver to put up the partition and turned to him, eyes filled with fury, pressing the pistol to Declan's face.

"I'm going to ask you this only once," Grant said now. "Did you let them go?"

Declan met Grant's gaze, struck by the absolute lack of fear he felt; there was only an eerie calm.

Grant had put Declan on guard duty, and he was out patrolling the grounds of the estate when Grant had taken the two American hostages. Unease and fear had gripped him once he'd learned what was happening; he knew he couldn't stand by and let Grant kill anyone else. His opportunity had come when Sorcha killed the lights. He'd heard the other guards shout that it was Sorcha who had gotten into the estate and escaped with the hostages. Hope had flared to life within him, and he knew exactly how she would try to escape. He'd dashed to the underground tunnel before the other guards could do so.

Declan had made his decision to stop following his uncle before he let Sorcha and the two Americans go. He'd probably made that decision the moment Wolfe had shot that driver in front of him, even though he hadn't realized it at the time.

He'd already begun to suspect that Grant was

lying to him about his motivations for finding the weapon; Finlay had only strengthened his suspicion. After speaking to Finlay, he'd snuck into Grant's private office and found documents confirming his uncle's true intentions . . . correspondence with weapons dealers and heads of governments known to sponsor terrorist activity.

His eyes were now wide open. Grant wanted to find the weapon and sell it for his own selfish means, regardless of how many people were killed in the process. He felt foolish for ever believing Grant's lies.

But now, if he wanted to get out of this alive, and get to his sister before Grant's men killed her, he needed to pretend he was still on Grant's side.

"No," Declan said, holding Grant's gaze. "You're wasting your time questioning me. We need to go after them."

Grant continued to glower at him, pressing the pistol even more firmly into his flesh; Declan knew it would bruise. But he didn't flinch, never breaking Grant's gaze.

Grant finally removed the pistol, twisting away from him, his expression still infused with rage.

"It wasn't Finlay. The American woman looked genuinely horrified to see her," he spat. "It had to be Sorcha who led them here. You're right, we do need to find her and the Americans. They'll just impede us. I'm going to give you one last chance to prove your loyalty. You will be the one to hunt down the treacherous bitch and her friends—and execute them. I want them to disappear with no traces of their bodies."

Icy dread filled Declan's chest, but he kept his expression neutral and offered a jerky nod.

"Two of my men will accompany you." He turned and leaned in close to Declan, narrowing his eyes. "Do not betray me, Declan. This is your last chance."

CHAPTER 19

Aberdeen, Scotland
10:38 P.M.

"hat do you mean—Excalibur is a place?" Adrian asked.

"I mean exactly that," Sorcha said. "Look, you keep talking about King Arthur and Excalibur, which is just a medieval myth," she said, waving her hand dismissively. "But beneath the myth, there is some truth. The Excalibur legend was always meant to protect a secret."

"This brotherhood," Nick asked, "what exactly is it? Does it exist to protect this secret?"

"Remember, we're on the same side," Adrian said when Sorcha hesitated.

"It's existed for centuries . . . back to the time of the druids, prior to the Roman invasion of Britain. My family has always belonged to the brotherhood, from me and Declan, our parents, our grandparents, and so on. Membership is generational, so there aren't many of us. One of the current leaders is my uncle, who I believe you had the pleasure of meeting," Sorcha said grimly, looking at Adrian. "Grant Macleod. So you see . . . it's a family affair."

"And this secret?" Adrian asked.

"The druids knew of a place, a deadly place, that could destroy the world. Where this place was or what it held that was so dangerous, that only a precious few knew of it, has been lost to time. But its importance has never faded, never been forgotten. This is the secret the brotherhood was created to protect. The secret it protects to this day."

Adrian sat in silence, still reeling at the knowledge that this weapon the brotherhood was protecting was actually a *place*—a place that still existed. At her side, Nick had paled.

"How can a place be a weapon?" she asked.

"We now believe it was some type of naturally occurring biological weapon, something the ancient druids didn't understand," Sorcha replied. "At some point in the past, the brotherhood—and I use that term loosely, as there are many women who are now a part of it—splintered into two groups," Sorcha continued. "There were always members of the brotherhood that wanted to find this place, and there was the part of the brotherhood that wanted to keep it secret, to protect the world from yet another deadly weapon. My brother and uncle joined the other side—let's call them the 'bad guys,' for simplicity's sake—after my parents' death. I've been working with the other side of the brotherhood, the ones who want to keep this place secret and hidden, like the ancient brotherhood wanted. A man named Michel Laurent is the leader of that side. James Poole was on our side," Sorcha added, her eyes filling with grief. "I was the one who asked him to follow you. He was vehemently against war and weaponry of any kind; he was a veteran who served in Afghanistan. He knew of the horrors of war. Even though he suffered from PTSD, he insisted on helping in any way he could."

"We went to James Poole's apartment to see if we could find anything useful," Adrian said. "We found a pendant there—that's how we found Grant's estate. Several men broke into his apartment while we were there. Mercenaries, I believe. We managed to hide while they were there. They seemed to be looking for something as well. One of them mentioned the name Richard. Do you know who that is?"

"Richard," Sorcha repeated slowly. "Richard Erickson. He works for Michel. Michel probably sent them to James' apartment to make sure there was nothing that could lead back to the brotherhood before the police did a search of his apartment. As for the pendant . . . it was a gift. My parents gave me and Declan ones when we officially joined the brotherhood. James lost his parents when he was still a boy, and they saw him as a bonus son. They gave him one as well." Sorcha lowered her gaze, her eyes filling with tears. "He was my friend. I only gave him easy tasks. I knew he was unstable, but I never . . ." She trailed off, tears filling her eyes as she pressed her hand to her mouth.

Adrian reached out to place her hand over hers. "What happened to Poole wasn't your fault."

"I never wanted anyone to die," Sorcha said, wiping away her tears. "That's why I went to Grant's estate alone. I knew it was risky, but I know how to use a gun; both my parents and Michel taught me when I was younger. I know my way around the estate, I spent part of my childhood there. I could have used Michel's resources, but I was trying to prevent more death. My plan was to wait until dark, slip into the estate, get the sword, and leave."

Sorcha expelled a shaky breath, taking a moment to compose herself. "Back to the weapon—to this place. You're probably wondering how all of this is connected to the King Arthur legend."

Adrian and Nick nodded, waiting for her to continue.

"Like I said before, peel back the layers of myth, and you get to the truth. Beneath the legend, there was a historical Arthur. And not just one. There were several . . . and they were members of the brotherhood."

"These historical Arthurs," Adrian said, stunned. "Who were they?"

"Riothamus, Ambrosius Aurelanius, and Owain Danwyn," Sorcha said. "Riothamus was a

Romano British general. He fought against the invading Goths on behalf of Rome. He lived in Brittany, which was a colony consisting of Britons who'd fled from invading barbarian armies after Rome fell. His link to the legendary Arthur was made by campaigns in France during which he led Britons into battle. Ambrosius Aurelanius was also a Romano British leader. He united his people to fight against the Saxons. Geoffrey of Monmouth, a medieval writer who popularized the Arthur legend, even directly placed Ambrosius into Arthur's story by making him his uncle. And then there is Owain Danwyn, lesser known than the other two. He was a Welsh king whose honorific title was 'Arthur'—which meant 'bear.' One of these Arthurs—historians aren't sure exactly who, as the leader is never named in the scant sources for the battle—led the Britons to victory at the Battle of Badon against the invading Saxons."

Adrian considered her words. It made sense that these historical figures would be behind the legend of Arthur. Like Arthur, they'd each united the Britons to fight against the invading armies of Saxons and other forces.

"And Excalibur?" Adrian asked. "Finlay told us some historical context for that particular legend," she added, bitterness filling her at the thought of Finlay. "She's working with Grant. Do you know her?"

"Yes. She's a member of the brotherhood. She comes off as quirky and offbeat, but I've always suspected that was a front. She can be cruel, and she's dangerously ambitious. I think she wants to lead the brotherhood for her own selfish purposes," Sorcha said, scowling. "As for Excalibur . . . the Arthurs did have special, intricate swords. The brotherhood exaggerated the importance and power of the sword to protect the secret of the actual *place* that was the weapon. By the time medieval writers wrote their version of the mythical Arthur, Excalibur was an indelible part of the legend."

"So . . . over the years, the focus of the legend became centered on the sword and not the place," Adrian said.

"Exactly," Sorcha said. "It was all a deception. All for the sake of protecting this place that could cause so much destruction. The swords that belonged to the Arthurs were believed to have messages inscribed on them, referencing the location of this place if it were ever needed—but only as a last resort." She looked up at Nick and Adrian. "That's why it was stolen, and why both sides of the brotherhood have been desperate to find it. Do you understand now? If the other side of the brotherhood finds this place—this biological weapon—it can kill millions."

CHAPTER 20

Inverness Airport
Inverness, Scotland
11:15 P.M.

Grant looked out over the tarmac where his private plane was waiting, preparing for takeoff. He clutched the box that contained the sword in his lap; he'd not wanted it out of his sight ever since the breach at the estate.

Anger coiled around him as he thought of Declan. The boy wasn't as good a liar as he thought he was. He had let Sorcha get away. *Such a shame.* Declan had potential, but he was never willing to do what was necessary. Yes, Grant had lied to him about what he planned to do with the weapon once he found it, but he'd foolishly assumed that Declan would eventually come around to his way of thinking. There was a weakness in him—just like his mother, Grant's sister, and her useless husband.

And that was why, like his parents, Declan had to be eliminated.

Declan's parents had been horrified rather than impressed when he'd told them what his plans were for the brotherhood, having the gall to threaten to go to the authorities. They'd left him with no choice but to hire a driver to run their car off the slippery M4 motorway one particularly rainy night.

Declan and Sorcha were young adults when their parents died, both at university. He'd hoped their adult children would do what was necessary to advance the brotherhood, but they were both weak, like their parents. His bitch of a niece had always been cold and distant toward him, but Declan had been more malleable. Grant never had children of his own, and with Declan he'd hoped . .
.

Grant shook his head as if to rid himself of the sentimental thought. He'd made his decision. He knew that Sorcha had to die, once she'd started searching for the sword and involving the police, but now Declan had to die as well. He'd appointed two men, including his most trusted mercenary, Wolfe, to accompany Declan to search for Sorcha; Declan was with them now. Grant had given them strict orders. Once they found Sorcha, both she and her brother were to be eliminated. It seemed, unfortunately, that Grant was the only one in their esteemed bloodline willing to do what was necessary.

Grant had inherited family money, his family's

wealth coming from the banking industry. But over the years, due to faulty investments and an erratic market, that wealth was rapidly slipping from his fingers. Once he found the weapon and sold it, not only on the black market, but to interested parties from several "controversial" governments around the world, he could regain that wealth—and more.

His motives weren't just financial. He wanted *more* for the brotherhood. Rather than hiding in the shadows, holding on to a worthless secret, they would have access to a weapon that could put them at an even level with some of the most powerful leaders in the world, with him as their representative, of course.

All he had to do was find the weapon, something the foolish ancient brotherhood had hidden, something that could have guided them out of the shadows, had they used it for their own means.

Grant would be the one to do it. He would bring the brotherhood to greatness . . . out of the shadows and into the light.

11:17 P.M.

ADRIAN PACED the length of the living room, rubbing her temples. "We need to get the sword ASAP. The police—"

"We can't trust the police. Grant has loyal

members serving both in the Aberdeen and Inverness Police Departments," Sorcha said sharply, shaking her head. "Michel believes that Grant may have one or more members working in Scotland Yard as well. That's why I was so adamant about keeping law enforcement out of this. I don't know who to trust."

"So we're on our own?" Adrian asked, heaving a sigh.

"We need to at least keep our boss back in the States in the loop. He can help where necessary," Nick insisted.

"If you trust him, and if he can remain tight lipped and only communicate with you," Sorcha said, after hesitating for a beat.

"Where do you think Grant has taken the sword?" Adrian asked. "There's no way it's still at the estate."

"No. My uncle is nothing if not paranoid. Knowing him, it's on his person," Sorcha said grimly.

"Where do you think he's taking it?"

"It could be anywhere," Sorcha said, closing her eyes in frustration. "My uncle has homes in Edinburgh, London, even the States."

They fell silent. Sorcha leaned back in her chair, looking deep in thought, while Nick's brow furrowed in concentration.

"Wait," Adrian said slowly. "We have an obvious link to Grant's part of the brotherhood. Declan."

She thought of the conflict in Declan's eyes. Declan could have easily killed or captured them, but he hadn't.

"I don't know," Sorcha said, pain tightening her features. "He's changed so much."

"He could have easily killed us, but he didn't," Adrian said.

"What are you thinking?" Sorcha asked, frowning.

"It's risky, but I think it's the only option we have right now if we want to find that sword," Adrian said. "Grant and his men have to be looking for us."

Sorcha nodded, bitterness flickering across her features. "My uncle likely has him searching for us now."

"Well," Adrian said, leaning forward, "let's help him find us."

CHAPTER 21

Aberdeen, Scotland
7:38 A.M.

Declan sat in the passenger side of the black Mercedes that Wolfe and another mercenary, Ben, had driven here in, watching his sister enter Westburn Park, silently cursing her for her stupidity.

Last night, he'd received a text from Sorcha, urging him to meet with her. He'd wanted to hide the text, but Wolfe had grabbed his phone and glared down at it, shaking his head in disbelief.

"The bitch must think we're dumb wankers," he'd said. "The police will be out in droves waiting for us."

"This is the best chance we have," Declan said, keeping his tone firm and cold. "We'll watch her from a distance at first, let them wait us out. But as soon as we have the opportunity, we grab her."

Wolfe looked at him for a long moment, briefly exchanging a glance with Ben. A dark look passed between them before they both nodded. "Fine. But if you don't do what needs to be done—"

"I know," Declan said shortly.

Declan wasn't a fool. He knew that in spite of his best efforts, his uncle still didn't trust him and likely had given them orders to execute both him and Sorcha.

Months ago, he wouldn't have believed Grant capable of such a thing, but he was no longer in denial about the depths of his uncle's cruelty. Declan's concern wasn't for his own safety. He'd brought this all on himself by choosing to join his uncle. He just wanted to protect his sister.

Now, as he watched Sorcha through a pair of binoculars, he scanned the park around her. There was no obvious sign of the police, or the two Americans, which just meant they were well hidden.

He glanced behind him at Wolfe and Ben, who were eyeing Sorcha as if she were the planned kill of a long hunt, making his blood run cold.

"We can take her out from a distance," Wolfe said. "I only need to get slightly closer, and—"

"No," Declan said quickly, hoping the panic didn't show in his voice. "I want to find out what she knows first."

"And if the cops take you down?" Ben asked.

"I'm willing to take that chance," Declan returned.

Not waiting for their response, he stepped out

of the car and headed toward Sorcha. It was too late to save his own life, but he hoped that he could still save his sister.

7:52 A.M.

Sorcha stood in the middle of the park, her heart hammering with nervous anticipation.

Adrian and Nick were seated in her rental car across the road from the park. Adrian had ordered her to run toward them if she sensed any danger from Declan and they would cover her. But Sorcha didn't fear her brother . . . it was whoever he was with that concerned her. She doubted Grant would send Declan after her, alone.

She'd convinced Adrian and Nick to not involve the local police. She didn't know who on the local force they could trust, or who could be in Grant's pocket. Adrian and Nick had only grudgingly agreed, but Nick told her he wouldn't hesitate to involve them if it came down to it.

Now, she looked around, anxiety coursing through her. She didn't know how long she had to talk to her brother, but she hoped she could get through to him.

One minute passed, then five. Then ten. She was starting to fear he wouldn't show when she saw a familiar figure approach from the opposite end of the park.

Declan.

As he drew near, she saw that his expression was hard, but there was something else lurking in the depths of his eyes. Fear.

"Dec," she said, as soon as he was within hearing distance. "Please, I just—"

"You shouldn't have come," Declan said, his voice low. "I was going to hold them off as long as I could. You have to get out of here—now."

"Come with me," she urged, reaching out to take his arm, but he took a step back.

"It's too late for me," he said, regret flaring in his eyes, "but I can at least get you to safety. I told Mum and Dad I'd always keep you safe, didn't I?"

Emotion filled her at his words. The loss of their parents was a shared grief that only they could understand.

"I'm getting you out of here, but I need you to play along," Declan continued. "Act like you're coming with me, but against your will. The police are with you, right?"

"No, just Adrian West and her partner. But, Dec—"

"Please," he interrupted. "Just come with me. Let me save you."

The desperate look he gave her made her relent. She swallowed hard and nodded, though she was still determined to persuade him to come with her.

But as soon as Declan grabbed her arm, jerking her to his side—a gunshot rang out.

It happened quickly. Too quickly.

In one instant, Declan was darting forward, shielding her from the bullet.

In the next, he was slumped on top of her, his body completely still.

CHAPTER 22

Aberdeen, Scotland
Two Minutes Ago

Adrian sat tensely next to Nick, watching from their secure vantage point from across the street as Sorcha started to walk off with Declan.

"What the hell is she doing?" Nick asked. "Are they—"

Before Nick could finish his sentence, a gunshot rang out.

Adrian watched in horror as Declan dove in front of his sister, the bullet striking him in the chest. The few passersby around them scattered and screamed.

Adrian and Nick were out of the car in an instant, racing across the street and into the park toward Declan and Sorcha. Adrian scanned the direction that the shot had come from and spotted two men darting toward a car.

Nick raced after them as Adrian hurried over to Sorcha and Declan. Sorcha was crouched over her brother, who was alive but dangerously pale, his breathing ragged. Blood seeped from the bullet wound in the center of his chest. Sorcha was weeping, pressing her jacket to the wound.

"Hold on, Dec, please hold on," Sorcha pleaded. She looked up at Adrian, her eyes wild with grief and desperation. "We have to get him help. I know a doctor I trust who can tend to him. Please, we don't have much time!"

∽

Aberdeen, Scotland
1:40 P.M.

ADRIAN SAT NEXT to Sorcha in the miniscule waiting room of a clinic. Sorcha was pale and shaking, her arms wrapped tightly around herself, while Nick paced before them. The shooters Nick had chased after had gotten away, and she knew their escape frustrated him.

They were in a clinic on the outskirts of Aberdeen. Inside one of the treatment rooms, Declan was being tended to by a doctor, Doctor Chris Stewart, who was a non-active member of the "good" side of the brotherhood, as Sorcha called it, and who had been a close friend of her parents.

They'd carried Declan to Sorcha's car and raced to the clinic in record time. Doctor Stewart had come out when they'd burst into the thankfully empty clinic, spiriting Declan into one of the treatment rooms with little explanation from them. He'd seemed to understand the breadth of what had happened by just looking at Sorcha's terrified face and Declan's wound.

Sorcha had told Adrian more about her and Declan's relationship. Their closeness until their parents' car accident, the shared grief that had briefly brought them closer before Declan distanced himself and joined Grant, and finally their estrangement.

"I should have fought harder for Declan and our relationship," Sorcha said. "I put my loyalty to the brotherhood over my own flesh and blood."

"I lost my father over ten years ago," Adrian said now, her heart clenching at the memory. "He went missing and is presumed dead. It's why I initially joined the FBI. I wanted to prevent other families from going through what me and my mother went through." Sorcha gave her a look of sympathy and they shared a silent moment, understanding what the loss of a parent felt like. "Not that it makes it any easier, but I would have wanted someone to share my grief with. My mother's sense of loss was different from mine. You're still his sister, and I can tell you still have a bond. It's not too late to repair what's been broken."

Sorcha fell silent, seeming to consider her

words. Adrian reached out to give Sorcha's hand a sympathetic squeeze, one which Sorcha returned.

Doctor Stewart came out of the treatment room, and Sorcha was immediately on her feet. He approached her, squeezing her hands and giving her a comforting smile.

"I managed to stop the bleeding. Your brother is very lucky. The bullet spared any major organs. Two inches to the left and—" He trailed off, shaking his head. "But he needs time to rest and recuperate." He gave Sorcha a long, meaningful look. "Is there somewhere safe where he can do that?"

"Yes," Sorcha said immediately.

"Then I would go there," Doctor Stewart said. He handed Sorcha a bag, adding, "Here are Declan's things. The nurse removed his phone and wallet."

Sorcha took the bag, thanking the doctor. She fished out his phone, studying it for a beat before tapping something. She swiped through the images on the phone . . . and froze.

"What is it?" Adrian asked.

Sorcha looked up at her and silently held out the phone. Adrian and Nick stepped closer to take in the images on the screen.

Adrian's pulse raced at what she saw.

Multiple photos of the stolen sword . . . along with close up shots of inscriptions beneath the hilt.

CHAPTER 23

Aberdeen, Scotland
6:32 P.M.

Adrian zoomed in on each photo of the sword on Declan's cell phone, carefully studying each Ogham inscription, Nick at her side.

Dating from the fourth century, Ogham was an alphabet that made up stone inscriptions now found on ancient stone monuments throughout the United Kingdom. There were many theories of its origin, from runes to the Latin alphabet, the latter of which most historians accepted. There were hundreds of inscriptions that still survived to this day. Appearance wise, they were diagonal, horizontal, or vertical slashes, relatively easy marks to make on stone.

They had returned to the apartment of Sorcha's professor friend in Aberdeen; Sorcha insisted it was the nearest and safest place, as

Grant and his cronies didn't know about it. Declan was in the master bedroom, resting, with Sorcha at his side. Sorcha, who was more familiar with Ogham than Adrian, had helped them decode the inscriptions after making sure that Declan was settled in.

Adrian focused on the first inscription, a series of slashes they had translated to the letters **I R T A** and **B A A L.** She and Nick had been brainstorming what these letters could mean but so far had come up empty.

"Adrian. Nick."

Adrian looked up. Sorcha hovered in the doorway of the master bedroom, looking nervous but relieved. "My brother is awake . . . and he's willing to talk."

Declan was sitting up when they entered. He still looked weak and pale, but otherwise remarkable for someone who had suffered a bullet wound.

At her side, Nick went tense, glaring down at him. She knew that Nick was itching to take Declan into custody, to do things the "proper" way. But given Sorcha's concerns about the local police being compromised, they had given Sorcha their word that they wouldn't involve them—for now.

"Are you sure we can trust him?" Nick asked Sorcha.

"Given that he's saved my life, and all of our arses back in Scotland, I'm going to say yes." Sorcha said, giving Nick a defiant look. "He also took photos of the sword—at great risk to himself —once he knew he was leaving Grant's side of the brotherhood."

Nick remained stiff. Adrian put her hand on his arm. "He's with us now, for better or worse," she said, giving Declan a firm look. "I assume we're after the same goal . . . stopping Grant from getting his hands on this weapon."

Declan gave her a confirming nod.

"We've been looking at the photos of the sword on your phone. Where is it now?" Adrian asked.

"With Grant," Declan said. "He told me he was heading to his home in Edinburgh, but I know he didn't trust me. He could've been lying."

"We've decoded the inscriptions, but they're just a series of letters. Do you know what they mean?" Adrian asked.

"No. Not even Grant knew. That's why he had Finlay and other experts there, analyzing them," Declan said.

"I've been looking at the inscriptions myself," Sorcha said with a sigh. "I'm just as stumped as you are. I have no idea what those letters could mean."

As Nick peppered Declan with more questions about Grant's potential whereabouts, Adrian thought about what the inscriptions could mean. She knew in her gut those inscriptions were vital. Sorcha had mentioned during the drive from the clinic that it looked like they'd been hidden beneath the hilt of the sword. The ancient brotherhood had taken great care to hide them.

She mentally reviewed everything she'd

learned about Arthur, Excalibur, the brotherhood, and this secret place it protected. She thought about the members of the ancient brotherhood engraving the sword with Ogham inscriptions, which were typically burial inscriptions.

Burial inscriptions.

An answer struck her with the force of a bullet.

"Ogham inscriptions are typically burial inscriptions," she said, interrupting Nick as she turned to face them.

"Yes," Sorcha said slowly.

"What if the ones on the sword are just that? Burial inscriptions for the Arthurs? You told us there were three historical Arthurs. What if the inscriptions are noting where they are?" Adrian asked.

"That could be the case, but the letters don't—" Sorcha began, but stopped herself. "Give me Declan's phone."

Adrian handed the phone to her. Sorcha looked down at the photos, shaking her head in disbelief. "Of course. I don't know why I didn't see this before." She looked up at Adrian. "The letters—I think they're out of order."

"I R T A," Sorcha continued, "that must be Riat, or the Pictish form of Riothamus' name, Riatev. The inscriptions must be in Pictish, even though most of the ones that have been found on stone monuments in the UK are in the primitive Irish language. Riothamus, like the legendary Arthur, was betrayed by a local ruler who was in bed with the enemy. And also, like Arthur, he died in— " She stopped abruptly, looking down at the inscription on the phone. "Avalon."

Adrian's eyes locked with Sorcha's as understanding dawned. She thought about the second set of letters they'd decoded. **B A A L**. She turned to Nick.

"The Celtic word for Avalon is Aballa. In Welsh the same word is 'Aval'. In Pictish, which is closely related to Old Welsh, it's 'Abal'."

"So the inscription reads Riothamus and Abal, aka Avalon," Nick said. "As in . . . the legendary Avalon?"

"Avallon—with two L's—is a very real place that still exists today, in France," Sorcha said. "Riothamus died near there. And this inscription is telling us that's where he's buried."

Adrian stood in silence for a moment, reeling. The inscription was proof that one of the men behind the Arthur legend died in a place that bore the name of the mythical island where his legendary counterpart perished.

"OK. So we need to go to real-life Avallon to find Riothamus' burial place," Nick said, shaking his head in disbelief. "But where do we even start looking?"

To her surprise, it was Declan who spoke. "Michel. He can help us."

Sorcha stiffened as she turned to face her brother. "Dec," she whispered. "Are you sure? The doctor said you need rest, and—"

"I can rest when we get there. Michel lives near the existing village of Avallon. He has the resources to help us narrow this place down," Declan said after a pause. He gave Sorcha a bitter smile. "Even if he does want to shoot me."

Sorcha studied her brother a moment longer before turning to Adrian and Nick. "Michel has a chateau in the Burgundy region of France. Like my brother said, it's not far from the actual village of Avallon."

"Then we know where we have to go," Nick said, straightening. "OK. Here are words I never thought I'd say . . . let's go to Avallon to find Arthur's burial place."

CHAPTER 24

Burgundy Region, France
10:55 P.M.

The Burgundy region, located in central France, had once been the Duchy of Burgundy before France annexed it in the fifteenth century. It was now filled with lush vineyards of Chardonnay, Pinot Blanc, Gamay, and other grape varieties that made its famous wines. Chateaus of various sizes also made up the landscape of the region, from old medieval castles to more recent ones from the nineteenth century on.

Adrian took in the rich landscape as the private car they were in weaved through the countryside. They were on their way to the chateau of Michel Laurent, the "true" leader of the brotherhood, according to Sorcha. Michel had arranged for them to fly privately from Aberdeen International Airport to Dijon-Darois Airport in France. A driver was waiting to take them to Michel's chateau, which was located just outside of Precy-le-Sec, France . . . ten miles north of the village of Avallon.

During the journey here, Sorcha had told her a bit more about Michel. He was from the *noblesse*, a French aristocratic family that had once hailed from Brittany before settling in the Burgundy region. Despite his family's wealth, he'd gone into business for himself, working his way up to becoming chief executive officer of an investment management firm before retiring the previous year. The entire time he'd been a silent leader of the brotherhood, as had his father before him, monitoring archaeological digs—and sponsoring a few—to seek the swords that belonged to the historical Arthurs.

"Michel and Grant were once friends, and though he's never expressed it to me, I know my uncle's decisions have devastated him," Sorcha said with a sigh.

Nick let out a low whistle as they arrived at a sprawling chateau, and awe swept over Adrian as well. It looked like something out of a fairy tale, with a white stone exterior and turreted roofs, nestled among sprawling gardens.

But her awe dissipated as soon as they stepped out of the car, when a half dozen armed men stormed out the front door of the chateau, surrounding them.

Panic swelled in her chest. They reminded her of the mercenaries who'd surrounded them at

Grant's estate in Scotland. At her side, Nick let out a groan and muttered, "I'm getting really sick of this happening."

"Michel!" Sorcha shouted. She didn't look fearful of the various guns trained on her; she just looked annoyed. "This is ridiculous. You knew we were coming. Tell these men to stand down."

After several tense moments, a man in his late fifties with gray-streaked dark hair and cool, intelligent eyes emerged from the front door of the chateau. His gaze swept dismissively over Adrian and Nick before focusing on Declan, who was hanging back, leaning against the car. Michel's expression went tight at the sight of him.

Michel ignored the rest of them as he approached Declan, who stood stock still, his face a hard mask, though he was still pale from his injury.

"I had my men on alert because I don't trust your brother," he said, addressing Sorcha, though his eyes remained on Declan.

"He saved my life," Sorcha hissed. "Twice. I told you this."

Michel continued to ignore Sorcha, his gaze trained on Declan. "Your sister wants to believe that you've changed. What should stop me from killing you now?"

Declan met his gaze evenly. "Nothing. I'll forever regret believing my uncle's lies. Sorch is all that I have, and I want her to be safe. So kill me if you have to. Just give me my word you'll protect her."

"No one is killing anyone," Sorcha protested, moving to stand protectively by Declan's side. "He's still recovering from the bullet wound he literally took for me, Michel. He needs to come inside and rest while we talk.

Michel seemed to waver, keeping his eyes locked on Declan before he came to some sort of internal decision. He turned to the men, focusing on a bulky, bald man with ice-blue eyes who stood front and center of the rest of the men.

"Jerome, it's OK," he said. "They can all stand down."

Michel turned to face Adrian and Nick. His lips turned up with the slightest hint of a polite smile, though he still looked guarded.

"Agent Nick Harper," he said, offering Nick a polite nod. "And you must be—in Sorcha's words—the irritating yet persistent Adrian West. Please come in. We have much to discuss."

London, England
11:02 P.M.

GRANT ENTERED the study of his London townhome, irritation coursing through him. He'd come to London instead of Edinburgh as he'd told Declan. He didn't trust his nephew, and it looked as if he'd been right not to. Grant was furious, though not altogether surprised that Declan had escaped with his treacherous niece.

Finlay and the two other historical experts he'd brought with him turned as he entered the study. Finlay looked pleased with herself, and Grant halted in his tracks.

"Please tell me you have good news."

"I do," Finlay said smoothly. He approached the table where the dismantled sword rested. Finlay pointed a gloved hand to the carved inscriptions. "We've decoded one of them."

Grant's heart picked up its pace as Finlay told him where it led . . . an actual village by the name of Avallon, in France. He looked at the other two historical experts, older men who'd looked down upon Finlay as soon as she'd arrived, but they grudgingly nodded their heads in agreement. He was about to ask about the other inscriptions when his cell rang. It was Wolfe.

"I just got a call from your man on Michel Laurent's security team. Your niece and nephew have just arrived at Laurent's chateau in France," Wolfe said. "What do you want me to do?"

Grant froze, delight swelling in his chest. All of his anger and frustration from just five minutes ago dissipated. He knew that Michel's chateau wasn't far from Avallon, which meant they must have come to the same conclusion that Finlay had.

Grant did the mental math, calculating how long it would take for him to fly to the nearest airport in Dijon from London, plus the drive. He needed to make sure they stayed put until then . . . he wanted to end his treacherous niece and nephew himself. It seemed fitting that he should be the one to execute them. Family was family, after all.

"Here's what I want you to do," he told Wolfe.

CHAPTER 25

Chateau Laurent
Precy-le-Sec, France
11:27 P.M.

Michel leaned against the edge of his desk, his arms folded across his chest as his gaze flicked from Sorcha to Declan, and finally to Adrian and Nick.

They were all gathered in the massive study of the chateau, Sorcha having just told him everything that happened since they'd fled from Grant's Scottish estate, ending with their conclusion about Riothamus' tomb being somewhere in or around the village of Avallon.

"What you've told me sounds feasible," he said. "But over the years, the brotherhood has already searched sites around Avallon, believing that one of the Arthurs' tombs may be there."

"Then those searches must have missed something," Sorcha insisted.

Michel still didn't look convinced. "And the other inscriptions?"

"We believe they point to the other two Arthurs—Ambrosius Aurelanius and Owain Danwyn," Adrian said. "But we're not as certain about their burial locations as we are about Avallon."

"As for Avallon, we just don't know exactly *where* to look," Sorcha added.

Michel moved over to a drink cart in the far corner of the study, pouring himself a tumbler of whiskey.

"When it comes to Arthur, I always like to start with the legend," Michel said, turning to face them. "What do we know about the legendary Arthur's burial?"

"The most famous tale is that he goes to the mythical Avalon after he's mortally wounded in battle with his nephew, Mordred," Sorcha said. "There are versions that have him surviving after being healed in this Avalon, while others—the one most people know—have him dying there."

"The enchantress Morgan le Fay ruled the Avalon of myth, along with nine sisters," Michel said. "We need to think beyond the legend, to the time during which our Arthurs actually lived. After the Romans left, many people of the British Isles returned to their Celtic roots, and that included their religion. A common feature of their religion was 'healing islands'—where, as the name suggests, people were sent for healing. Can you guess who would often keep watch over such islands?"

"Priestesses," Adrian said slowly, already seeing the parallels.

Michel nodded. "Exactly. There are historical mentions of such healing islands, including one by a Roman geographer by the name of Pomponius, who describes an island of the River Elorn, inhabited only by priestesses, including an oracle for a Celtic god. He notes that there are nine in number." He raised his eyebrows. "Sound familiar?"

"So healing islands were common during the time of the historical Arthurs?" Nick asked.

"Indeed," Michel replied. "Now, circling back to Celtic religion. Bodies of water were a very important aspect of it. The Celts believed that water was the realm of the gods. They would throw votive offerings into bodies of water as offerings to their gods; it's the reason we throw pennies into fountains to this day," he added. "Turning back to the legendary Arthur—think of the lady of the lake. Want to take a gander where she came from?"

"Celtic water goddesses," Adrian said, shaking her head in amazement.

"Exactly. Old pagan shrines have been discovered on islands dedicated to goddesses such as Cliodna, who was a lake goddess; Slioch, a water goddess, and other water deities. Of course, our tale wouldn't be complete without the rise of Christianity," Michel continued. "What did the Christians do when they came across pagan shrines or temples? For the most part, they simply turned them into churches, abbeys, monasteries. It was easier for the newly converted to stomach worshiping at temples that they were familiar with and had already existed for centuries."

Adrian leaned back in her chair, understanding where Michel was going with this. And by the look on his face, Nick understood as well.

"So Riothamus is buried at or near a church that used to be a pagan temple dedicated to a water goddess . . . one that could have been part of a healing island," Adrian said.

"I believe so," Michel confirmed. "We need to take a look at Christian churches or old temples that are within or near Avallon."

Michel got up, moving over to one of the study's cabinets, entering a code to unlock it. He took out several rolled-up maps, spreading out one of them on the desk. At their look of surprise, he gave them a rueful grin.

"I'm rather old school when it comes to maps. Besides, these older ones pick up historical nuances that even Google Maps miss."

Adrian chuckled, thinking of her friend Sebastian Rossi, who also insisted on keeping analog versions of everything digital. She stepped forward, along with Nick, Sorcha, and even Declan, who had been lying down on the couch at Sorcha's insistence. They all took in the large map that Michel unfurled and placed on his desk.

"There are several churches that could possibly fit," Michel said. "But I'm thinking the most likely candidates are these." He took a pen and marked off four locations on the map. "They're near small bodies of water—one a small lake and the others narrow streams."

Adrian looked down at the churches, her heart hammering with hope. Could one of these churches contain what they were looking for?

"Ideally, I'd like to go during the day, but I know it's important to find this place quickly," Michel said. "Since there's several of them, I suggest we—"

His words were interrupted when the windows of the study shattered, sending shards of glass exploding inward as bullets peppered the room.

CHAPTER 26

*A*drian dove to the floor, along with Nick and the others. Just outside the windows of the study, she could hear the shouts of Michel's men and returning gunfire.

Her blood turned cold. Grant had found them.

"Stay low!" Michel cried out over the cacophony. "Follow me!"

Clutching the maps and moving in a crawling position, Michel scrambled toward the doorway; Adrian and the others were right behind him.

To her horror, once they got outside of the study, she saw the body of one of Michel's guards just outside the doorway.

"Oh my God," Sorcha whimpered.

Adrian looked around, taking in the empty hallway, her body tense. She wished she had any type of weapon on her. Michel, who had gone pale at the sight of the body, swallowed and composed himself.

"This way," he said, turning to head down the hallway away from the study.

They followed him, all on sharp alert. Michel halted as a man who Adrian recognized as his main guard approached from the far end of the hall.

"Jerome," Michel said, relieved. "Thank God. We—"

But Jerome silenced him by lifting a pistol and aiming it at them, his expression cold. Adrian stiffened, alarm coursing through her.

"On your knees," he barked.

Michel just looked at him, horrified. "Jerome—"

"I won't repeat myself," Jerome snapped.

Adrian watched in disbelief as Sorcha stepped forward, ignoring Declan's restraining hand on her arm. "It's my uncle, isn't it?" she spat. "You're working for him?"

For a moment, Adrian couldn't believe Sorcha's bravery—or stupidity—as she stepped toward Jerome. But then she saw Sorcha give them a quick look. It reminded her of the look she'd given her back at the estate in Scotland. While that look had been one of warning, this one was a signal to act.

Adrian darted forward, using Jerome's distraction with Sorcha to her advantage. She lowered her body to kick out at Jerome's knees as Declan and Nick charged toward him as well.

Nick tackled him to the ground, dislodging Jerome's pistol from his hand, slamming his head on the ground several times, hard, rendering him unconscious, while Declan grabbed his pistol.

Adrian whirled, panicked, when she heard the front door to the chateau crash open, more shouts, and footsteps pounding toward them.

"Follow me!" Michel shouted, darting down the hallway.

They obliged, and Michel led them into a massive kitchen, moving toward what looked like a tall cabinet. He pressed a button on the side, and to her amazement it slid open to reveal a narrow, bare-bones room. A makeshift panic room.

"Inside. Hurry!" Michel hissed.

The footsteps were getting closer. Adrian and the others darted inside just as several men raced into the kitchen.

Michel entered the panic room, slamming a button next to the door as the men hurried toward them. The door slid shut slowly—too slowly—just as one of the men reached the door, raising his weapon to fire—

The door slid shut just in time. Adrian closed her eyes, relief sweeping over her, though it was only short lived. They couldn't stay in here forever.

Michel moved past them, opening a sealed cabinet next to another door in the rear of the room by entering a code. It slid open, revealing a rack of car keys, along with several guns. He reached for one set of keys, handing them to Sorcha, before giving Nick, Declan and Adrian each a weapon. He then handed Sorcha the rolled-up maps he'd taken from his study.

"Those are the keys to the Bugatti," he said.

"And the maps, they cover France and all of the UK. They should help in your search for the tombs. Take the back entrance."

"You're not coming with us?" Sorcha asked shakily, taking the keys.

A crash sounded against the door and Michel turned to face it, his mouth set in a grim line.

"I need to buy you time."

"Michel—" Sorcha protested.

"He's right," Declan interrupted. He turned to face Michel, and something silent yet intense seemed to pass between them as the men locked eyes.

"Go. Now," Michel said, moving to the rear door, entering another code. The door slid open, leading to a set of stairs. "This leads down to the garage."

Sorcha reached out to give Michel a quick embrace before heading out, Declan giving him a nod before following her. Adrian and Nick followed suit, thanking him before descending the stairs after Sorcha and Declan. She could hear bullets ricocheting off the door of the panic room as Michel slid the door shut behind them.

At the base of the stairs was a spacious garage filled with several high-end cars; Sorcha led them to a sleek black Bugatti. They all climbed in, Adrian and Nick taking up positions in the back seat, Declan taking the passenger's side, their weapons at the ready as Sorcha started up the car.

As soon as the engine roared to life, and the

garage door slid open, two men burst into the garage. Sorcha floored the accelerator, peeling out just as the men fired off several shots.

Once they were out of the garage, another car was immediately on their tail. Sorcha let out a curse and sped up. Gunshots pierced the exterior of the vehicle as Adrian, Nick, and Declan returned fire.

"Is there another road we can take?" Adrian shouted, as the men behind them fired off more shots.

"There's one—but it's on the other side of that forest," Sorcha said, jerking her head to the left. Adrian saw a patch of trees off the side of the road.

"Then that's where we need to go," Adrian returned. "Nick, Declan, aim for their tires! We need to buy time."

"Right ahead of you," Nick said, leveling his gun at the pursuing car. Declan followed suit, and they both fired off several shots, aiming right for its tires.

The pursuing car careened off the road, and Sorcha swerved the Bugatti to the left, racing toward the trees.

CHAPTER 27

Chateau Laurent
Precy-le-Sec, France
1:45 A.M.

Grant stormed into the grand drawing room, his blood boiling as he took in his former friend Michel, who sat kneeling in the center of the room, his face battered and bruised, the barrel of a gun placed against the side of his head by Wolfe.

While he was en route from London, flying privately from London's Heathrow Airport to the Dijon-Darois Airport, his men had secured the chateau, wiping out the small security force Michel had on the grounds. But his errant niece and nephew, along with the two American federal agents, had still escaped.

He gestured for Wolfe to step aside, taking out his own pistol and pressing it to the side of Michel's head. To his irritation, when Michel met his eyes, there was no fear there.

"Where did they go?" Grant hissed.

Michel said nothing. Grant raised his pistol, slamming it down on Michel's temple. Michel crumpled to the floor, but merely got back up again, his expression neutral.

"I'm only going to ask you one more time," Grant snarled. "Where. Are. They?"

Michel just looked at him, a flicker of sadness in the depths of his eyes. "There was a time I would have called you a good man, Grant," he said. "What happened to you?"

Michel's words caused fury to spread through Grant. He had always been so bloody self-righteous.

"I'm taking the brotherhood out of the shadows and into the light," he said, and pressed the trigger.

Burgundy Region
France
1:52 A.M.

ADRIAN EXAMINED one of the maps Michel had given them, as Sorcha made her way down a narrow road that wound through the Burgundy countryside. Nick and Declan were in the back seat, their weapons out, scanning the road behind them.

Since escaping from the chateau, they'd gone to two other churches on the map, with no luck. The first one was locked with no way to access it, and the other one no longer existed.

They were on their way to the third church on the map, but Adrian was losing hope. Since Grant and his men were now in the area, they could know about Riothamus' burial site being somewhere around Avallon . . . and beaten them to it.

"Here we are," Sorcha said, her headlights picking up a decrepit church on the side of the road up ahead. Sorcha looked tired and shaken; Adrian knew she was terrified for Michel, but was trying to focus and keep her composure.

"Let's hope the third time's the charm," Nick said grimly.

Sorcha parked the car behind the church so that it was out of sight from the road.

They piled out of the car and made their way inside. The interior of the church was even more decrepit than its exterior, consisting of crumbling stone floors and partially collapsed pews. A thick layer of dust and cobwebs covered every surface.

Covering her mouth and nose with her shirt, Adrian ventured farther in, looking around. Toward the rear of the church, she noticed a stone slab resting on the floor.

They headed toward it. Adrian squatted down, examining it. It was covering a square opening beneath it.

"Let's move this—there's something under here," she said.

Together, using all of their collective strength, they pushed the stone slab aside. Beneath it, the opening led to a set of stairs that descended to a cellar below.

Using her cell phone flashlight to guide her, Adrian made her way down the stairs, the others close behind. The stairs were surprisingly steady despite the decaying state of the church.

Cracked stone floors and crumbling brick walls made up the cellar, with an even thicker layer of dust coating everything in sight. They coughed, covering their noses and mouths, using their cell phone flashlights to illuminate the space.

But there was nothing that stood out. It was just a dilapidated, empty cellar.

Defeat settled over Adrian—until she noticed something.

She stepped closer to the wall to her left, noticing that one brick seemed slightly misshapen from the others. It looked . . . off.

"Guys," she said, and the others approached, Sorcha shining her light on the brick.

"It's different from the others," Sorcha confirmed.

Nick and Declan stepped forward and pressed against the stone to dislodge it, but it wouldn't budge.

Adrian gritted her teeth, frustration filling her. "Stand back."

"Adrian," Sorcha protested, as Adrian aimed her pistol. "Wait. What if—"

But Adrian had already fired.

The brick crumbled, dislodging the other bricks around it. Adrian and the others stumbled back as the collapsing bricks revealed a small opening.

Sorcha gasped. Roughly a dozen feet inside the revealed space . . . there was a pile of bones.

Pulse racing, Adrian swept her light over the bones, freezing when she shined it on the ceiling directly above the bones.

There was an inscription carved there.

CHAPTER 28

They all took in the bones, and inscription, in silent awe.

Adrian stepped forward, studying it. The inscription was written in Latin:

INTER MAGNA SAXA TERRAE
DORMIENTIS

"Between the great rocks of the sleeping land," Adrian translated, reading out loud.

"Well, way to be specific," Nick muttered after a lengthy pause. "That could be literally anywhere."

Sorcha and Declan stepped forward, studying the bones closer.

"From what I've seen on digs, I'm going to guess that this was a male in his mid-forties," Sorcha said. Her eyes swept around the space surrounding the bones. "He was likely buried with funerary items—jewelry, weapons, armor. If he had a similar sword to the one we found in Dorset, it would have been here as well. Grave robbers must have gotten here years ago."

The sound of an approaching car's engine suddenly came from above the cellar. Adrian froze before her hand flew to her pistol; they all stood stock still until the sound of the car passed them by.

Adrian's shoulders sank with relief, but tension still hummed throughout her body. The historian part of her wanted to stay and examine the bones, to alert the local historical authorities, but the other side of her knew it wasn't safe for them to stay here for long. Grant's men could be on them at any minute. When this was all over, she knew Sorcha would make certain to have a team of archaeologists comb over the site. By the hungry look in the other woman's eyes, it would probably be Sorcha herself supervising the survey.

"We need to get somewhere safe while we figure out this inscription," Adrian said.

"I know where we can go," Sorcha replied, finally tearing her eyes away from the bones.

Dijon, France
7:48 A.M.

Sorcha gazed out at the view from the balcony of her room in the bed-and-breakfast.

The city of Dijon sprawled out before her, with its medieval terracotta roofs and the spiraling tower of the Dijon Cathedral in the distance.

The capital city of the Burgundy region, Dijon, was filled with a mix of architectural building types that attested to its varied history, from Renaissance to Gothic. The Dukes of Burgundy had once ruled from here during the medieval era, when the city was one of the great centers of art and science in Europe. Now it was a charming medieval city, popular with tourists for its wine, gastronomy, and historical sites.

She'd suggested they come to Dijon; it was the closest city with a large enough population for them to blend into rather than one of the smaller villages in the Burgundy countryside. And most importantly, it had an airport.

Adrian had readily agreed with her. Ever since Adrian had comforted her about Declan, confiding in her about what had happened to her own father, Sorcha felt a growing camaraderie with the other woman. They shared commonalities . . . they were both historians, they had both suffered parental loss. And now they were allies in trying to stop Grant's side of the brotherhood from finding the weapon.

Sorcha and the others had gotten two adjoining rooms, but Sorcha had barely slept, her stomach twisted into knots over worry for Michel. Declan had also been awake throughout the night, even though she insisted he needed his sleep for his continued recovery. He had still spent much of the night tossing and turning.

She'd tried calling Michel's secret emergency number, but there was no answer. She had a terrible feeling in the pit of her stomach; it was the same feeling she'd had when her parents had died. Tears burned behind her lids, and she blinked them back.

How had everything gone so wrong? James had died, Michel was possibly gone, and now her uncle was on the verge of finding the secret the brotherhood had worked for centuries to protect. She felt the weight of failure pressing down on her shoulders, and took a deep, shuddering breath to calm herself.

"Sorch."

She turned to find her brother standing behind her, studying her with concern.

"You should be lying down."

"There's only so much lying down I can do. The meds Doctor Stewart gave me have been doing the trick," Declan said. He leaned against the railing, studying her. "You're worried about Michel."

It was a statement, and not a question, but she nodded anyway.

"So am I," he confessed. He heaved a sigh, regret shadowing his features. "I never should have joined Grant. I really thought I was doing the right thing. Michel used to believe in me, but after I joined the other side . . ."

"He was just hurt," Sorcha said, reaching out to squeeze his arm. "You're like a son to him. He could have had his men kill you, no matter how much I protested. But he could tell that you were being truthful."

Declan seemed to consider her words for a moment before continuing. "I told myself that I was joining Grant for our family's legacy. But really, I was being selfish. I needed a distraction from my grief. The more lies Grant fed me, the more I ate them up, even though I knew deep down that something was wrong."

"The past doesn't matter now, Dec. You're on the right side now." She reached out to squeeze his hand, a renewed surge of determination coursing through her. "And we *will* honor our family's legacy—and that of the brotherhood's—by stopping Grant."

7:55 A.M.

Nick hovered just outside the balcony, watching as Adrian leaned against it, her eyes closed, head tilted toward the sky, something she did every time she was in deep thought.

Watching her now, he recalled the desire that had roiled through him when they were both in the crawl space back in James Poole's apartment, her curves pressed tight against him. He'd cursed himself for thinking with his nether regions when they were in so much danger, but the attraction he'd felt toward Adrian had long been simmering beneath the surface.

He and Adrian were sharing a room, with him insisting on taking the couch while she took the bed. They had shared rooms before when they were partners, but this time felt . . . different. For one thing, it surprised him how comfortable he felt spending the night in the same room as Adrian after all this time. For some reason, it just felt right, and he didn't have the mental bandwidth at the moment to examine his feelings around why.

"Still take your coffee black?" Nick asked, deciding to make his presence known as he joined Adrian on the balcony.

Adrian's eyes flew open as Nick stepped out onto the balcony with two cups of coffee, giving him a grateful smile.

"I do," she said, taking the cup he handed her with gratitude. He knew she was bone tired and hadn't slept much; he didn't think any of them had after the events of yesterday.

"I'm guessing your sleep was like mine," Nick said, taking a sip of his coffee. "Shitty."

"Yep. I just hate feeling like we're missing something," Adrian said with a sigh. "It's a persistent feeling I had nearly the entire time we were in Egypt for the Cleopatra case."

"Well, let's take everything apart," Nick said, leaning against the balcony next to her, looking out at the horizon. "The Ogham inscription on the sword led us to that tomb. I think it stands to reason that the inscription we found at the tomb leads us to the next place, which is quite possibly *the* place."

Adrian nodded her agreement. Nick thought again of the inscription. *Between the great rocks of the sleeping land.*

Adrian abruptly set down her coffee. At Nick's questioning look, she said, "This is all about the brotherhood. We need to use the two members of the brotherhood that are right next door to help figure this out. I'm going to take a guess that they're as awake as we are right now."

CHAPTER 29

*A*drian had barely knocked when Sorcha swung open the door to her room. She smiled and stepped aside to let Adrian and Nick enter.

"Is it significant that there are three inscriptions?" Adrian asked, as soon as she and Nick were inside. That had been a fact that niggled at her . . . the three Arthurs, the three inscriptions. It all seemed deliberate.

"The number three is significant to the brotherhood," Sorcha replied. "The earliest founding members of the brotherhood were druids—Celtic priests. The number three was sacred in Celtic religion. There were triadic deities, such as the Morrigan. There was also the Triskele, a triple spiral symbol of the Celts going all the way back to Neolithic times."

"There even used to typically be three leaders of the ancient brotherhood," Declan added.

"If that's the case," Adrian said, "and there are two other tombs, it stands to reason that there are two other inscriptions like the one we found last night. And once we put all three together—"

"They'll tell us the location of the place," Sorcha concluded, nodding her head in agreement. "Of course. That makes sense. It's a way the ancient brotherhood had to make certain that the right person finds the location of the place. Only the most trusted would have all three." She closed her eyes, rubbing her temples, a look of worry flashing across her face. "We have to move fast. We don't know where my uncle, Finlay, and his other men are on this."

Adrian sat down on the edge of one of the beds, frowning in concentration. She thought about the other letters of the Ogham inscriptions, the ones linked to the other two Arthurs.

"The other two inscriptions on the sword are also likely to lead to the burial places of the other Arthurs. What do we know about their last days?" Adrian asked.

"Well, not much is known about Ambrosius Aurelanius' last days, but we do know that a descendant of his ended up ruling over a kingdom in Brittany," Sorcha said. "So it's likely he ended up fleeing Britain when the Saxons made their successful incursions inland, like many Britons did at the time. If not, a descendant of his—or a member of the brotherhood—could have buried him in Brittany to be closer to his family."

"Who was this descendant who ruled in Brittany?" Nick asked

"Conomor. He lived in Domnonee, which is now the Brittany region of France," Sorcha replied.

"Dol," Declan said slowly. They turned to look at him. He straightened, stepping forward. "That's the inscription next to Aurelanius' name on the sword. It's out of order, written as L D O."

"Oh my God," Sorcha breathed, meeting her brother's eyes. She turned to face Adrian and Nick. "One of the communes in modern day Domnonee is Dol-de-Bretagne. It was known as Dol historically. If Aurelanius' family eventually settled there—"

"Then that's where he's buried," Adrian said, her heart picking up its pace. "OK. We have one potential location. What about Owain Danwyn's last days?"

"Owain died in battle around the year five twenty," Sorcha said. "He died not far from the capital city of his own kingdom of Powys. In sixth century Britain, warriors who fell in battle near their family burial plots would have been interred there. So I think it's likely he was interred with the royal family of Powys."

"Where is that?" Nick asked.

"The inscription on the sword next to Owain's name is A S B," Declan reminded them.

Sorcha straightened, pacing, before halting in her tracks. "Bas," she said. "Bas—for Baschurch." She whirled to face them. "The kings of Powys were buried at a place called *Eglwysau Bassa,* Old Welsh for churches of Bassa. There's a village in England called Baschurch, and it's had that name since ancient times. But that's not all," Sorcha continued. "There's a hillock near the village called Berth Hill. Historians believe it was a ceremonial compound, based on early archaeological surveys. It was in use when Owain died."

Hope filled Adrian at Sorcha's words. They now had two likely locations for the next two tombs, though if they were wrong about both or even one of the locations, they would lose precious time.

"I think we should split up into two groups; one goes to Brittany, the other to Baschurch," Adrian said finally.

"Really?" Nick asked, wary. "Splitting up never works in horror movies."

"Adrian's right," Sorcha said. "What if we're wrong about one or both locations? We speed up the process this way. Declan and I will go to Baschurch. I have some contacts at a local museum there who can give me answers."

"Then Nick and I will head to Brittany," Adrian said. "Let's hope that we're going to the right places—and that we beat Grant there."

CHAPTER 30

Dol-de-Bretagne, France
1:17 P.M.

Dol-de-Bretagne was a quaint French village in the Brittany region of northwestern France, situated above marshes that hugged the coast. Medieval homes and buildings along with winding cobblestoned streets filled the village, which was known for its grand thirteenth-century cathedral, the Cathedral Saint-Samson.

Adrian and Nick had flown from Dijon to Rennes, then driven forty-five minutes north to Dol-de-Bretagne from the Rennes Bretagne Airport. Using one of Michel's older maps, along with their modern electronic maps on their phones, they made their way on foot to the outskirts of the village, just past the main road that meandered throughout it. According to Michel's map, there was an old church there by the name of Eglise de Champs, a church that had been built over the ruins of a temple to a Celtic water goddess.

But when they reached the location noted on the map, Adrian halted in her tracks. The church they were looking for hadn't been on their modern maps, but Adrian had assumed it was because it was an old ruined church, like the one they'd found near Avallon.

Nothing stood where the church should have been.

Nick muttered a curse as Adrian double checked Michel's map, but they were in the right place. She closed her eyes, frustration surging through her. There were no other viable churches in the area for them to check; the area beneath the famous Cathedral Saint-Simon had already been thoroughly excavated.

Had they wasted precious time by coming here?

"I suggest we harness the power of the locals. They'll know more about this church—or any other potential church we can look for—in this area," Nick suggested.

Moments later, she and Nick had made their way to the Museum of Dol, the local history museum. As they entered, a smiling elderly woman greeted them in French at the front desk. She introduced herself as Honorine.

"We were hoping to see the ruins of the old

church, the Eglise de Champs," Adrian responded in French.

"Ah, that was unfortunately torn down around fifty years ago."

"Oh," Adrian said, trying to hide her growing frustration behind a polite smile. "That's disappointing. My husband and I are history buffs interested in former pagan temples in the area. I believe there was once a temple there before the church was built? Do you know if they found anything when they tore down the church?"

"I'm not certain," Honorine replied with a frown. "We do have photographs and records from that time. Give me a moment."

When Honorine returned ten minutes later, she had a small stack of documents with her. "You're in luck," she said, beaming as she slid them toward Adrian and Nick.

Adrian looked down at the documents, which were copies of photographs. Her heart leapt into her throat as she flipped through them.

The photos were ruins of an old temple, along with several close-up shots of an old, worn-down inscription.

"According to the notes with those photos, the archaeological survey team believed there may have been a tomb or some sort of burial space there at some point," Honorine said. "But it was long gone by the time the church was torn down."

Adrian was barely listening, her gaze trained on

the inscription. Though they were faint, she could make out the words in Latin, the only part of the inscription that was legible.

AQUAS FLEUNTIBUS

Running waters. Somehow, it paired with the inscription they had found near Avallon.

Adrian met Nick's eyes, a palpable wave of excitement passing between them.

She turned to Honorine, trying to maintain her composure as she offered a polite smile.

"Is it possible for us to get copies of these?"

Berth Hill Museum and Historical Society
Baschurch, England
1:32 PM

SORCHA ENTERED the Berth Hill Museum and Historical Society, Declan on her heels, hoping she looked more confident than she felt.

Sorcha had already spoken to the head curator, Louisa Fletcher, on the phone before she arrived, telling her she needed to look at records from archaeological surveys in the area, specifically ones carried out at Berth Hill. She had met Louisa on one occasion before, during a dig she'd carried out not far from Berth Hill. She could only hope that

Louisa wouldn't be too suspicious of her vague reasoning for needing to look at the records.

When she and Declan arrived at the front desk, Louisa, a handsome woman in her fifties, approached them with a polite smile.

"Doctor Manning," she said, giving Declan a nod after Sorcha introduced them. "I don't mean to be difficult, but I checked with the British Museum after we spoke, and they had no knowledge of your visit."

Declan tensed at her side, and Sorcha forced herself to keep her smile pinned on her face. She'd forgotten how by-the-book Louisa was.

She'd just have to go with a half truth.

"The museum wanted to keep my visit under wraps. I'm working with Scotland Yard on"—she lowered her voice—"the recent theft of the Dorset artifacts."

Louisa's eyes widened in surprise, but she still looked uncertain.

"Let me speak to the head of the archives, and then we can—"

"That won't be necessary."

Ice flooded Sorcha's veins as she heard the distinctive rumble of her uncle's voice behind her. She and Declan whirled.

Grant entered the lobby, flanked by several of his men and Finlay. He held the terrified middle-aged security guard by his neck, his gun pressed to the side of the man's temple.

Rather than looking angered at finding Sorcha

and Declan there, a delighted smile spread across Grant's face.

"If it isn't my niece and nephew," he said. "I've been wanting a family reunion."

CHAPTER 31

Berth Hill Museum and Historical Society
Baschurch, England
1:54 P.M.

Sorcha stood next to Finlay at the front desk, huddled over the records that a shaken Louisa had provided them with—at gunpoint.

She tried to ignore Grant and his men, one who stood next to her, his gun leveled at her, and another who stood in front of her, with Declan on his knees, his gun pressed to the side of his head. Grant himself paced restlessly before them, periodically shooting her a glare.

Terror flooded her veins, and her hands shook. She forced herself to take a calming breath. Grant's men had shepherded the other employees and visitors of the museum to a back room; she could hear their terrified whimpers from here.

Grant had ordered her to work with Finlay to comb through the museum records to see if there were any hints of a tomb located in Berth Hill. Needless to say, it was difficult to concentrate. When she'd come here to look at the records, she'd hoped they would reveal any markings or inscriptions found in the area during early archaeological surveys of the area.

But other than a few funerary items with undecipherable markings and shards from pottery and no-longer-standing stone monuments . . . there was nothing. She had the gnawing feeling that the tomb they were looking for wasn't here, and that she'd been too hasty in her assumption that the inscription on the sword led here.

But she wasn't going to let on to Grant what she suspected. She needed to remain useful to her uncle to keep herself and her brother alive.

Her cell began to ring, and she stiffened with alarm. That had to be Adrian or Nick.

Grant, who had confiscated her and Declan's phones, immediately fished it out of his pocket. He looked down at it, his expression darkening.

"It looks like your American friend is calling," he said. He stalked over to her, answering it and putting them both on camera. He looped an arm around Sorcha's shoulders, smiling widely as Adrian's shocked face appeared on the screen.

"Hello, Miss West. It's good to see your lovely face again."

Dol-de-Bretagne, France
2:15 P.M.

ADRIAN'S BLOOD ran cold when Grant's face appeared on the screen, a visibly terrified Sorcha at his side.

She and Nick had left the museum and were in the local library as they reviewed the records that Honorine had given them. She'd wanted to fill Sorcha and Declan in on what they'd found.

Adrian shot to her feet, panic, anger, and fear coursing through her. Nick did the same, his face going pale.

Before she could speak, Grant continued, "My niece and nephew are gathered with some of our friends here, the employees of the Berth Hill Museum, along with some visitors. I suggest you and your boyfriend work with me . . . unless you want me to start killing people."

Adrian's panic swelled, but she forced herself to remain silent. At her side, Nick had gone tense, but he also kept silent. He knew what she did: men like Grant liked to be in control. They needed to pretend to give him that power.

"So," Grant said, "I want to know what you've found, both in Avallon and wherever you are now—the location of which I'd very much like to know. Now, please."

Before Adrian had a chance to respond, Grant

whirled the cell phone's camera around, lifted his pistol, and shot a security guard who was tied up on the floor. The guard slumped over, his eyes wide and unseeing.

Shock coiled around Adrian as Nick let out a curse, and hostages in the background screamed. He turned the camera back to his face, giving her a wintry smile.

"Just an incentive for you to know that I'm not bluffing. Now start talking."

She met Nick's eyes, and he gave her a subtle nod. They didn't have a choice; Grant had proven that he wouldn't hesitate to kill if they gave him false information.

"We're currently in Dol-de-Bretagne in France. Outside of Avallon, we found the remnants of a tomb we believe may have belonged to Riothamus, along with an inscription: 'Between the great rocks of the sleeping land'. We've just discovered another inscription in Brittany that's degraded, but from what we can tell, it reads 'running waters'," Adrian said tightly, hating every word that she forced past her lips.

"Good girl," Grant said, giving her a condescending smile. "Now, there's an address I want you and Agent Harper to go to, just outside of Rennes. I want you there in exactly forty-five minutes. If you show up with any authorities, or if any police show up here, I *will* kill everyone in this bloody museum."

CHAPTER 32

Berth Hill Museum and Historical Society
Baschurch, England
2:20 P.M.

Sorcha's blood thrummed in her ears, fear constricting her throat. She was unable to take her eyes off the dead security guard, or the blood soaking the ground around his body.

She had long accepted that her uncle was evil. She knew that he'd killed before—hell, he'd tried to have her killed. But to see it happen right in front of her...

"I suggest you snap out of it and concentrate," Grant snapped. "Or your brother is next."

Sorcha blinked, giving Grant a hasty nod. Finlay, who didn't look remotely concerned with the dead body of the guard, had taken out a piece of paper and written down what Adrian had told Grant, studying it with concentration.

"Between the great rocks of the sleeping land. Running waters," she said, shaking her head. "That's incredibly vague. It could point to anywhere."

Sorcha had to work to keep her expression neutral, to hide her disgust. Sorcha and Declan were being held at gunpoint, an innocent man had just been murdered, and there were terrified hostages in the back room. Yet Finlay was acting like this was just a scholarly exercise.

She took a steadying breath, finding determination through her grief and anger. She had to keep Grant's murderous hands away from the place the brotherhood had strove for so long to keep hidden.

With this in mind, an idea struck her.

A dangerous idea.

Before she could talk herself out of it, she abruptly reached for one of the photos from a file, pretending to take great interest in it. Finlay studied her, frowning.

"What is it?"

"I think I may have found something," Sorcha lied.

∽

Rennes, France
3:02 *P.M.*

ADRIAN DROVE toward the small farmhouse on the outskirts of Rennes, her hands clutching the steering wheel in an iron grip. She had driven here from Dol-de-Bretagne in record time, terrified that Grant would start killing hostages at will.

As she drew closer to it, she could see why Grant had chosen this location. Fields surrounded the farmhouse on all sides, with no glimpses of any other homes or buildings nearby.

It was isolated enough for Grant's men to easily execute and dispose of her and Nick's bodies.

She looked over at Nick. Though his entire body radiated with tension, he gave her a reassuring nod. A sudden rush of gratitude that Nick was at her side swept over her. Her partner. They had faced life-and-death situations before, and if there was anyone she was walking into such a situation with again, she was glad it was him. Impulsively, she reached out to take his hand, allowing the warmth that spread through her at his touch to permeate. He squeezed her hand in return.

Together, they'd made a hasty plan on the way to Rennes, one she prayed worked. They didn't have any other options.

Taking a deep breath, Adrian turned onto the dirt path driveway that led to the farmhouse.

Two of Grant's men emerged from the farmhouse and approached, their guns out and at the ready. Adrian's pulse thrummed beneath her skin; she swallowed hard as she eased the car to a stop but kept the engine running, holding up her hands. Nick did the same.

The men approached cautiously, their guns

raised. They were shouting at her in French to cut the engine. Adrian frowned, acting as if she couldn't understand them, keeping her hands raised.

As the men got even closer, Adrian made her move.

She pressed down on the accelerator. The car lurched forward, but both men darted out of the way just in time.

Bullets pierced the back window, causing it to shatter.

"Get down!" Adrian shouted. She jerked the car in reverse, racing backward, ducking as several more bullets pierced the rear windows.

She heard a thud as one of the men bounced off the rear of the car. Only then did Nick jerk open the passenger side door, leaping out as Adrian continued to veer backward.

The second man turned on his heel, trying to outrun her car. She jerked the car to a stop as Nick darted into her path, slamming his body into the man.

Adrian reached for the only weapon she had access to, the car's tire iron that she'd set aside before making the drive down here. Scrambling out of the car, she whirled toward the first man she'd hit, but he lay sprawled out on the ground, unconscious.

She turned her focus to Nick, who was still fighting the second man. She raced toward them, slamming the tire iron down on the man's head. He let out a howl of pain as Nick grabbed his gun, pinning him to the ground with his knees, pressing the weapon to the man's forehead.

"We'll let you live, asshole," Nick snarled. "But you have to do something for us first."

CHAPTER 33

Berth Hill Museum and Historical Society
Baschurch, England
3:10 P.M.

Declan could tell that Sorcha was up to something.

Wolfe gripped him roughly by the arm, his gun now jabbed into Declan's side. Remnant pain from his bullet wound spread throughout his body, and he fought to hide his grimace. From the vitriol pouring from the man, Declan knew Wolfe was aching to shoot him.

Declan was doing the best he could to ignore Wolfe, his entire focus on Sorcha. His sister had certain tells when she was lying; her eyebrow would twitch and her lips would turn down. As Sorcha spoke to Finlay, he could tell that whatever she was telling her was lies.

As if feeling his eyes on her, Sorcha looked up,

giving him a brief look that told him everything he needed to know. *Be ready.* It was the same conspiratorial look they shared whenever they were hiding something from their parents as kids. Only this was much more serious.

He remained perfectly still, keeping his expression neutral. It was important that he not show any emotion. Grant's men had once been his colleagues, and he knew they saw him as a traitor. A few weeks ago, this would have devastated him, but not anymore.

He knew the chances of him getting out of this alive were slim. The only reason he was alive now was because Grant needed Sorcha's cooperation.

His gaze landed on the spot where Grant had shot the security guard. Grant's men had carried the body off, but his blood still soaked the ground. Declan tried not to think about how much the guard reminded him of the young driver that Wolfe had killed in cold blood the night he stole the artifacts. He still saw the young man's fearful face and lifeless eyes in his nightmares . . . he doubted he would ever forget the man's face. How could he? His blood was on Declan's hands.

Declan briefly closed his eyes, recalling his sister's words. *That's all in the past. You're with us now.* His penance would be to get Sorcha and the other hostages to safety, he was just at a loss as to how. He hoped Sorcha had a damn good plan.

Grant's phone suddenly shrilled, and he answered, his face softening in pleasure as he listened to the voice on the other end. He hung up, approaching Sorcha and giving her a wide smile.

"Your American friends have been handled by my men. We don't have to worry about their interference anymore."

Declan's heart lurched, and Sorcha paled. She closed her eyes, pressing her fist to her mouth; she was stifling a sob. After several moments, she opened her eyes, which were now filled with determination.

"I think I've come up with something," Sorcha said, her voice shaky. "If I tell you, will you let the hostages go?"

Grant reached out to grab Sorcha's jaw, and Declan instinctively lurched forward. Wolfe immediately punched him in the gut, making Declan keel over in pain.

"Do you really think you're in a position to negotiate?" Grant snarled.

"Yes," Sorcha said, keeping her gaze steady on Grant's face. "You need my knowledge. I won't feel secure telling you what I know if anyone else is killed."

Grant studied her for a long moment, his mouth tight with anger.

"Before we—*negotiate*—tell me what information you have," he snapped.

"I know where the next tomb is," Sorcha replied, not missing a beat.

Sorcha was becoming an eerily good liar.

She'd lied to the police in London during the investigation of the stolen artifacts. She'd lied to the Scotland Yard detective about Adrian West. Before that, she'd essentially lied for years by keeping her involvement with the brotherhood a secret.

But this lie was to keep herself, and others, from getting killed. Once she'd outlasted her usefulness, her uncle would kill her and Declan. This lie, of all the ones she'd told before, was the most crucial one she needed to sell.

In the photos from the archaeological surveys, Sorcha had noticed that there were fragments of ancient stone monuments that were no longer standing. There were markings on them, but they were so degraded that they were mostly undecipherable. The inscriptions could either be runic markings, Ogham inscriptions, or even Latin words.

She was going to use their indecipherability to her advantage.

"These inscriptions," she said, pointing them out to Grant and Finlay in the photos, "they belong to stone monuments that once stood in the area, likely burial markers. The markings on them are badly degraded, but I can make out runic markings that show the word 'king' and another that indicates 'Bassa.' There's a smaller hillock just to the west of here known since ancient times as Bassa Hill. There are the ruins of an ancient pagan temple right by it that's already been surveyed, but I think something was missed. I think that's where Owain may have been buried instead."

"You don't think he's buried at Berth Hill? Then why did you come here?" Grant demanded, his eyes narrowed.

"The same reason you did. I *thought* it was the right place. But based on these inscriptions, I'm thinking I was wrong."

Grant turned to Finlay, who was studying Sorcha closely. If anyone could see through her bluff, it was Finlay. She didn't like the woman, but she clearly knew her stuff.

Finlay studied the photos for several long moments while Sorcha held her breath.

"These markings are hard to make out, but I can see how she came to this conclusion. From what I've seen in the records, I don't think our Arthur is buried at Berth Hill. It's too different from the burials of the other Arthurs. The ancient brotherhood was consistent. I think they would isolate his tomb on its own, so he's likely buried elsewhere."

Relief flooded Sorcha. She also believed Owain was buried elsewhere based on Finlay's same conclusion, but she'd lied about the Bassa Hill connection. She figured this was Finlay's confirmation bias at work. Finlay already doubted they were looking in the right place, which just played into her hands.

To her further relief, Grant seemed satisfied by Finlay's answer, turning his focus back on Sorcha.

"You'll take us there, but I'll be in constant communication with my men here. If you're deceiving me, I will kill several more hostages in your name. Do you understand?"

It took everything in Sorcha's power not to flinch, to not think of the risk she was taking with people's lives.

But she had to do something.

"I understand."

CHAPTER 34

Ten Miles West of Baschurch, England
4:12 P.M.

Sorcha was very aware of the pistol that Grant had pressed into her back as she led them toward the woodland that surrounded the hillock that was Bassa Hill. She'd been to this area once, several years ago, for an archaeological survey. She prayed she'd made the right choice in location; it was where she planned to make her escape with Declan.

Grant had brought Declan with them, as she suspected he would, to keep her at heel. He didn't realize that Declan being here was a crucial part of her plan. Declan had his own man on him, a scary-looking bloke who went by the name of Wolfe, along with Finlay.

Sorcha tried to keep the appearance of calm as she led them into the small patch of forest that led toward the hillock. She didn't know exactly when she was going to make her move; she just knew that she needed to get them deep enough into the forest that she and Declan had a viable means of escape, to flee back to Grant's car and somehow alert the authorities without getting the hostages back at the museum killed.

Her heartbeat was thundering in her ears as she led them deeper into the forest, drawing closer to the hillock. The crumbled ruins of the old pagan temple were roughly twenty meters to the south of it. As soon as it came into view, she would make her move.

The rising hillock soon appeared in the distance, along with the old temple. Sorcha struggled to maintain her calm, though she felt as if her heart were going to catapult out of her chest.

"There," she said, stopping to point at the temple. "Do you see it? It's right near the base of the hill, to the left."

"I see it," Grant snapped, shoving the pistol into her back. "Walk."

Sorcha obediently took several more steps—and made her move.

Using the element of surprise to her advantage and moving faster than she ever had in her life, she whirled, shoving Grant as hard as she could. Startled, Grant's hands went up, the pistol flying out of them.

Behind them, Declan had already taken action.

He reared back and head-butted Wolfe, who stumbled back.

Sorcha leapt forward, grabbing the pistol off the ground, but Grant slammed into her from behind, knocking the air from her lungs, causing her to loosen her grip on it.

Grant shoved Sorcha onto her back, lifting up his fist and slamming it into her face. Sorcha's head whipped back, her temple throbbing with pain. Grant straddled her, his face a mask of fury.

"You treacherous bitch," he snarled. He snatched up the pistol, pressing it to the side of her face. Sorcha struggled to twist away, panic strangling her. *I'm going to die.*

But a bullet struck Grant's shoulder from behind, sending him lurching forward. And then Declan was there, shoving Grant's limp form off her and helping her to her feet. She stumbled into his arms, still woozy from Grant's blow. Over Declan's shoulder, she could see that Wolfe lay on the ground, blood soaking the ground around him, a bullet wound in the center of his chest.

Behind them, they heard a twig snap. They both turned toward the sound. In the melee, she'd nearly forgotten about Finlay, who'd clearly taken flight.

"Stay here," Declan barked, and charged after Finlay.

Sorcha ignored his order and followed, though she couldn't run nearly as fast as her brother, still disoriented and in pain from her tussle with Grant.

She glimpsed Finlay up ahead, scrambling forward as fast as she could, but she was no match for Declan, who tackled her to the ground.

Sorcha reached them, gasping for breath, as Declan aimed the pistol at Finlay.

Shaking, Finlay held up her hands in surrender.

～

Rennes, France
4:51 P.M.

A FLOOD OF SURPRISE, relief, and suspicion filled Adrian as her cell rang, the caller ID indicating that it was Sorcha who was calling.

After Nick made Grant's surviving mercenary lie to his boss and tell him that he and Adrian were dead, they'd left him securely tied up back at the farmhouse, making a call to the police before leaving.

They were now on the way to the airport, trying to figure out how to free the hostages without alerting the authorities and putting all their lives in danger.

As the phone rang, she looked at Nick, whose expression was just as conflicted as she felt. Uneasy, she answered, placing the call on speaker and on camera, just in case it was a trick from Grant.

Sorcha and Declan's bruised faces appeared on

her screen, and Adrian gasped with relief. She found a side street and pulled over.

Sorcha and Declan looked just as relieved to see them.

"Thank God," Sorcha breathed. "I was praying that Grant was bluffing about killing you."

"I'm not so easy to kill," Adrian said, smiling. "Neither is my partner. What happened?"

Sorcha told them everything that had happened from entering the museum to the moment they'd managed to escape. Declan had shot Grant, and they'd left him tied up in the forest, along with his dead mercenary, Wolfe, while they tied Finlay up in the same area. Declan had made Finlay call off Grant's men at the museum before they'd called the police. They had left Grant bleeding out and was uncertain if he was still alive; their focus had been on making certain the hostages were freed and getting the hell out of there before Grant's reinforcements came.

Adrian's gaze strayed to Declan; his face was shuttered. Given that Declan had killed Grant's mercenary, he could have easily killed his uncle as well. She suspected he couldn't bring himself to do it, despite everything his uncle had done. She knew that Declan didn't share his uncle's murderous nature.

"During the whole ordeal, I realized the tomb we're looking for isn't at Berth Hill," Sorcha was saying now, her face filling with regret. "There was nothing in the records indicating any type of similar inscription to the ones we've found. Those who are buried there are likely members of the royal family from that time period. The Arthurs, however, are buried individually. I was too hasty in jumping to conclusions. I'm familiar with the Berth Hill complex, so I was operating off of my own confirmation bias."

Adrian leaned back in her seat, considering this.

Thus far, the two lines of the inscription they'd discovered weren't terribly helpful in determining where this dangerous place was located. She suspected the third line, the one they were missing, was crucial to figuring it out.

She studied the weary expressions of Sorcha and Declan, surprised at the kinship she now felt with them, two people who had recently been a suspect and an enemy. She could tell they were fiercely determined to stop Grant's side of the brotherhood from finding this weapon, a determination she shared. The only way they were going to find this next place was by working together, and she'd feel better—and safer—if they were all in the same location.

"We'll find it," she said. "But first, let's meet up somewhere safe."

CHAPTER 35

Shrewsbury, England
9:20 P.M.

Grant's eyes fluttered opened, taking in the cold, sterile room he was in. For a moment, he wasn't certain where he was or how he'd gotten here . . . until everything came flooding back to him. The hostages he'd held in the museum. His niece leading him to that hillock. The ambush. The gunshot.

At the memory of the gunshot, Grant winced, reaching up to touch his shoulder, which was securely bandaged. He sat up in the narrow cot he was in, grimacing in pain, as Finlay entered.

At the sight of her, red-hot rage poured over him. He recalled her fleeing during the ambush, not even attempting to help him or Wolfe. He should have killed the bitch. Finlay seemed to sense his rage, but didn't look perturbed as she approached him.

"Before you say a single word, you should know that you would have bled out if it weren't for me," she said matter-of-factly. "Your lovely niece and nephew left me tied up for the police. I managed to not only escape my bonds, but I got to you and called one of your mercenaries for help. This is a clinic just outside of Shrewsbury. We had to pay the doctor here a hefty fee for his discretion." Her gaze went to his shoulder. "That might hurt like a bitch, and despite your heavy bleeding, it turned out to just be a flesh wound. Your nephew could have easily killed you, but for some reason, he didn't."

Grant stiffened as he thought of Declan. A small, foolish part of himself was disappointed that Declan hadn't tried to kill him. It again proved to Grant what he already knew, that Declan wasn't capable of doing what was necessary to achieve the brotherhood's goals. It was something Grant would remind Declan of before he put a bullet into his foolish skull. A final lesson.

"You ran when they attacked," he continued, ignoring her earlier—and valid—point about saving his life.

"I'm not one of your mercenaries," she said with a shrug. "I'm not a fighter or a killer. It's better that I did . . . I don't think Declan would have hesitated to kill me. He killed Wolfe, after all. And again, I saved your life."

He studied her with narrowed eyes. True, she was no mercenary, but she wasn't a kindhearted woman. As much as she irritated him, he admired the cold-bloodedness that seemed to run through her veins.

"Why did you? Save me?" he asked, his voice edged with suspicion.

"Because I need your resources, resources that will be hard to access if you're dead. And after I tell you what I'm going to tell you, I'm going to need . . . assurances."

"Assurances?"

"Yes. I want a sizable cut of the proceeds from profits you make when we find this location. I also want to share in leadership of the brotherhood. Starting with its name, of course. A bit of a misnomer," she added, gesturing at herself.

"And why would I give you such assurances?" he asked in disbelief.

"Because while you've been out—even during you niece's bullshit field trip—I've been thinking. And talking to your other experts. I've figured out where the next tomb is. The one that will lead us to the destination the old brotherhood tried so hard to keep secret."

He studied her. After Sorcha's latest betrayal, he was wary of trusting anyone, but Finlay wasn't Sorcha. She only acted out of pure self-interest. She knew he wouldn't hesitate to kill her if she betrayed him; there was nowhere she could go to escape him. And she had taken the effort to save his life. Given her need for assurances, she was as invested in this as he was.

"Fine," he said shortly, knowing that he ultimately didn't have to give in to her demands. Once she served her purpose, he could just kill her.

"I'm not your foolish niece and nephew," she said, her eyes narrowing, as if reading his thoughts. "Retaliate against me, and there will be consequences."

He glared at her, though a reluctant surge of admiration swept over him. Perhaps he had underestimated Finlay Morrow.

"You have my word."

~

Manchester, England
9:45 P.M.

"You're absolutely certain that the Berth Hill complex was the wrong place? That the tomb we're looking for isn't there?" Nick asked Sorcha, his expression wary.

They were gathered in a room in a hotel adjacent to Manchester's airport, where they had agreed to meet up. It was only an hour-and-a-half drive from Baschurch, where Sorcha and Declan were coming from, and a two-and-a-half-hour flight from Rennes. They'd determined it was best to meet somewhere close to an airport or train station since they'd need to leave at a moment's notice after figuring out the location of the next tomb.

"Ninety percent," Sorcha replied. "What I saw in those records didn't track with the other two tombs."

"Ninety percent isn't one hundred percent," Nick said with a scowl.

"She's doing the best she can," Declan said, frowning. "Cut her some slack, mate."

"I just want to make sure we're not wasting our time," Nick snapped.

"Bickering isn't going to help us find the next tomb," Adrian interrupted.

She stood from where she was leaning against the small desk in the corner of the room, moving to stand in between Nick and Declan, who were glaring at each other. While Nick had overcome his initial distrust of Declan, there was still some lingering tension between them, unlike the camaraderie she and Sorcha had developed.

She'd also noticed during their time together that the momentary interest Sorcha seemed to have in Nick when they'd first met had dissipated; Nick certainly had shown no interest in Sorcha. Perhaps it was because of all of the tumult they'd been through since Scotland, but it relieved Adrian all the same, even though she told herself it was none of her business.

"Let's go back to the legendary Arthur's story again," Adrian said. "We know about him going to

Avalon after he's mortally wounded in battle. Where does this battle take place?"

"Camlan, according to the Welsh tradition," Sorcha replied. "Some scholars think that Camlan could also mean Camelot."

"Is there a real-life counterpart to this Camlan? Akin to modern-day Avallon in France?" Adrian pressed.

"There is a valley in Wales called Camlan," Sorcha said, after considering for a moment.

Adrian stepped forward, looking down at Michel's maps that they'd spread out on the floor. She picked up the map of Wales, studying the area near Camlan Valley, thinking of the letters inscribed in Ogham next to Owain's name on the sword. A S B.

Her gaze landed on an area marked Abas Hills.

"Abas Hills," she said, looking up at the others. They moved closer, studying the map over her shoulder.

"It's near three rivers, right at their junction—Afon Cywarch, Afon Cerist, and River Dyfi," Sorcha said slowly.

"According to this map, there was a temple dedicated to a Celtic river goddess near here," Adrian added.

"This area used to be a part of the kingdom of Powys . . . Owain's kingdom. If his solo tomb is going to be anywhere, it would make sense for him to be buried there," Sorcha said, her voice rising in excitement.

Hope surged through Adrian as she studied the map and the three rivers near Abas Hills. She recalled how the number three was sacred to the ancient Celtic religion, and therefore, the ancient brotherhood.

This could be the final piece of the puzzle they were looking for.

CHAPTER 36

Dinas Mawddwy, Wales
12:26 A.M.

The village of Dinas Mawddwy in Wales was surrounded on all sides by nature, nestled within the confines of Snowdonia National Park. With the mountain of Foel Dinas looming to the west of the village, along with the rolling green hills and lush greenery of trees that surrounded it, Dinas Mawddwy looked like it belonged on a postcard.

Adrian drove through the village, maneuvering the car through the narrow streets. During the two-hour drive from Manchester, they'd brainstormed, trying to determine where the two inscriptions could possibly lead to in case their trip to Wales ended up in a dead end, but came up with nothing concrete. Adrian could only pray they would find what they were looking for here.

She made her way to the western edge of the village, where their destination lay: a picturesque stone church, not far from the junction of the rivers.

Adrian parked, taking in the brilliant starry night sky that stretched above the village. She could imagine an ancient temple once standing here, lit by torches from Celtic priests. Had members of the ancient brotherhood buried Owain here?

They piled out of the car, Adrian looking around cautiously as they approached the church. As they drew closer, Adrian froze, catching the sight of a shadow behind the church.

"Get down!" she screamed, as several gunshots rang out.

Adrian and the others dove to the ground, using the car as cover as bullets rained down around them.

Panic, anger and frustration filled her. Grant's men had gotten here before them, and had lain in wait, knowing they were coming.

They took out the guns that Declan had confiscated from Grant and his mercenary back in Baschurch. Adrian and Nick cautiously peered out from behind the car. There appeared to be just two men who were firing at them, crouched down behind the church.

More shots fired out, ricocheting off their car, and Adrian and Nick took cover once more. They returned fire, but Adrian knew their ammunition wouldn't last forever.

Adrian noticed that one shooter abruptly disappeared. Fear lurched through her as she realized he was going around to the other side of the church.

"Cover me!" she shouted.

"Adrian—what the hell are you—" Nick began, as Adrian darted out from behind the car, dodging gunfire from the other shooter.

Behind her, Declan, Nick and Sorcha returned fire as she raced toward the other side of the church, her pulse racing. As she drew closer, she could hear the man moving through the brush behind the church.

She forced herself to go absolutely still, and as the shooter emerged from behind the church, his weapon raised—

Adrian aimed her gun and fired, striking him right in the chest. He went down.

She whirled, finding Nick, Declan, and Sorcha advancing toward where the other shooter had just stood. She joined them, noticing that the man was now darting toward a parked car in the near distance. He must have realized that he was now outnumbered.

They raced after him, Adrian and Nick firing off shots, but he dove into his car and sped off.

Nick let out a curse as Declan studied the retreating car.

"I recognize him—that's Isaac. One of Grant's men."

"Grant must have survived, and both he and

Finlay got away. She figured this location out before we did," Sorcha said with frustration.

Adrian noticed the look of guilt that flickered across Declan's face before it shuttered again. Her assumption was correct; Declan hadn't been able to kill his uncle. He looked away from her penetrating gaze.

"Guys," Nick said. He gestured to the back doors of the church. Someone had shot the handle off and the door was partially open.

They entered cautiously, weapons drawn, making their way into the back room of the church, which appeared to be a records room with stacks of books and documents piled onto bookcases. A partially open door stood at the far end of the room.

They approached it. Adrian pushed open the door, peering inside. The door led to a small staircase that descended into a dark, narrow tunnel below.

Together, Adrian and the others cautiously made their way down the stairs, using their cell phone flashlights to guide them.

They ventured down the tunnel, which was surprisingly long. Adrian gripped her weapon just in case someone else was lying in wait for them. The longer the tunnel stretched, the more nervous she became.

But the tunnel came to an abrupt end. Right next to where it stopped, on the left wall, there was a circular opening. She could see bullet holes penetrating the wall around it. Grant's men must have shot at it, akin to what she'd done at the church in France, to get the wall to crumble.

The opening revealed a spacious area of six by four feet inside . . . an area that could have easily once been a tomb. Yet it was completely empty.

Adrian expelled a frustrated sigh, stepping back.

"Wait," Nick said, squatting down and shining his light on the ceiling of the empty tomb. "There's something here."

Adrian squatted down next to him, her eyes going wide when she saw what he'd noticed.

It was faint, having partially eroded away, but there was a legible inscription there, written in Latin.

AB ORIENTE VENERUNT MONI-
TIONEM MORTIS

"From the east they came, bearing a warning of death," Adrian read aloud.

The sudden sound of footsteps behind them caused panic to spiral through Adrian. She turned, lifting her pistol, ready to fire.

But it was a petite, elderly woman who approached, her expression tight with alarm as it swept over them. As soon as her gaze landed on Sorcha and Declan, she let out a gasp, her face going pale.

"Sorcha and Declan. It is you," she breathed. "You both have the look of your mother."

Adrian and Nick stiffened with surprise. Sorcha frowned, hesitantly stepping forward as Declan reached out to hold her back.

"Who are you? How did you know our mother?" Declan demanded, his voice hard with suspicion.

"They were members of the brotherhood, as am I," the woman replied. "Given the shootout I heard, and the dead body outside, you must be as well. And," she added, looking meaningfully at the opening behind them, "I do believe I know why you're here."

CHAPTER 37

Dinas Mawddwy, Wales
1:15 A.M.

"I was a member of the brotherhood in my younger years. I still consider myself a member, just not an active one. Like your family, my family has belonged to it for generations," Agnes said.

The woman, who'd introduced herself as Agnes, had taken them from the church to her cottage. Her cottage was only a couple of miles away from the church; they were now nursing cups of tea in front of a roaring fireplace in her living room.

Agnes told them she'd come to the church to fetch some urgent paperwork she'd left behind, when she'd seen the shootout and watched the other gunman speed off. She'd approached them only after recognizing Sorcha and Declan.

"I had a young family when I chose to no longer be active, though I continued to help keep knowledge of the weapon a secret," Agnes continued. "I work at the church doing general administrative work."

"Did you know that the ruins of Owain's tomb were there?" Adrian asked.

"No. Myself and other members suspected it was in the area, but I had no idea it was literally right under my nose—for years," Agnes said, looking abashed.

Sorcha set down her tea, leaning forward. "Our uncle, Grant Macleod, is the leader of the other side of the brotherhood, the part that wants to find the weapon and exploit it for their own means. His men got to the church before we did. We need to stop him from finding it."

"We've found the two other inscriptions," Adrian added. "'Between the great rocks of the sleeping land', 'running waters', and this final line: 'From the east they came, bearing a warning of death'. Do you know what they could all mean?"

"No. It's intentionally vague," Agnes replied. "The ancient brotherhood didn't want just anyone figuring out the location."

"Between the great rocks . . . that has to mean mountain ranges," Declan offered. "So . . . a valley?"

"There are countless valleys all over the UK," Sorcha pointed out.

"And running waters—a river? Stream?" Nick added. "Again, they couldn't have been more vague if they tried."

"We're thinking in general terms," Adrian said. "We need to be more specific." She turned to Sorcha, Declan, and Agnes. "Think of everything you know about the early brotherhood. Who was the first to speak of this place? This weapon?

"It began with the druids," Agnes replied. "They were the founding members of the brotherhood."

"Where did they get it from?" Nick asked.

"No one knows, but there are theories. Local tribes moving in and out of the region, possibly the druids themselves, coming from some other location," Agnes replied.

They all fell silent. Adrian leaned back in her seat, studying the crackling flames in the fireplace. She thought about the ancient Celts who'd settled in the United Kingdom, migrating from continental Europe. Some of them must have possessed the knowledge of a place so dangerous, it needed be kept secret for centuries.

Again, she ran over the three lines of the inscription in her mind. *Between the great rocks of the sleeping land. Running waters. From the east they came, bearing a warning of death.*

She stiffened, thinking of that last line. *From the east.*

"Sorcha, what do you know about the migratory patterns of the Celts? I know the common theory is that they came from continental Europe, but where exactly?" Adrian asked.

"The most accepted theory right now is that they migrated from central Europe, around the Danube River," Sorcha replied.

"According to the inscription, we're looking for somewhere to the east, and given how far back in history all of this goes, I think it's safe to assume it's not the eastern part of the UK," Adrian said. "I think we need to go *further* back in history. Where else could the Celts have come from?"

Sorcha leaned back in her seat, considering, when Agnes spoke.

"There are tales," Agnes said slowly, "of the Irish who came from the east."

"The Irish from the east?" Nick echoed.

"There's a blood disorder that's common in Ireland—haemochromatosis. My late husband had it. It's nicknamed the Celtic disease. I remember doing some research into it. Historians believe, based on genome analysis, that it was brought by people from the east, specifically the Pontic Steppe, which stretches into Russia from Bulgaria, thousands of years ago."

"I remember hearing about this," Sorcha said, nodding. "A few years ago I attended a conference about links the modern Irish share with Ossetians, a tribe in southern Russia. Ossetians are descended from Scythians, who eventually made their way west, intermixing with the Celts. There are cultural similarities between the Ossetians and the Celts—reverence of horses, the spiral ring design we often think of as Celtic or Irish. The Ossetians also used totem poles carved from oak, something the Celts did as well. The druids revered oak; it was their sacred tree. And," Sorcha added, "there's also the round table."

"The round table?" Nick spoke up, his eyes going wide. "As in—"

"The legendary Arthur and his knights, yes," Sorcha said. "It's something that many Ossetian households have as a symbol of friendship and hospitality."

Adrian considered their words, thinking of a tribe of Celts coming from Russia. She closed her eyes, drawing on her specialty—historical linguistics. She thought of all the language families in the region, several of which she was familiar with. There was Turkic, Mongolic, Northwest and Northeast Caucasian . . .

Sleeping land.

"I'm going to assume this region is remote," Adrian said, thinking aloud.

She thought of the ancient languages of the region, running through them in her mind until she landed on Tatar, spoken by the indigenous peoples there.

Sleeping land.

Adrian jumped up from her chair, knocking over her tea. The others looked at her, startled.

"Sleeping land," Adrian breathed. "That's from

the Tatar language, or rather a dialect of the language—Siberian Tatar. In that dialect, 'sleeping land' literally translates to Siberia."

CHAPTER 38

They all sat in stunned silence for a moment before Nick spoke.

"Siberia," he echoed. "OK. But where in Siberia?"

Adrian closed her eyes, her mind racing, recalling every word of the inscriptions. *Great rocks.*

"Great rocks," she said aloud. "That has to be a clue as to the name of the mountain range. What mountain ranges pass through Siberia?"

Sorcha took out her phone, opening a map of the region. She zoomed in, studying the various mountain ranges.

"There's the Ural Mountains, the Skalisty Range, the Chersky—"

"Skalisty," Adrian interrupted, her heart hammering. "That's the Russian word for 'rocky.' Between the great rocks . . . that has to be the Skalisty Range."

"And 'running waters'—that can narrow it down even more. That has to reference a river or some body of water nearby," Nick added.

Adrian turned to Agnes. "Do you have a computer we can use?"

Moments later, they stood gathered around Agnes' laptop monitor, studying a map of Siberia they had zoomed in to focus on the Skalisty Mountain Range.

"There," Declan said, pointing to a river that wound through the northwest part of the range. "The Tompo River."

Adrian studied the map; the area still covered a lot of ground. They would need to narrow it down even further, but she knew in her gut they had the right place.

She turned to face Sorcha and Declan; what she was going to say next wouldn't be popular.

"We won't be able to locate the precise location on our own," she said. "And if Grant has already found it, he's going to use all his resources. We need to bring in our own resources. It's time to loop in Scotland Yard and the FBI."

Events had moved at such a frenetic pace that they hadn't been in contact with Briggs since flying to Grant's estate in Scotland, which now seemed like ages ago.

Adrian braced herself for their protests, but they both gave her reluctant nods of agreement.

"At this point, we have no choice," Sorcha said,

expelling a sigh. "We *have* to get there before Grant. Millions of lives are at stake."

∼

London, England
2:34 A.M.

DCI JACK STEVENS paced the small space of his kitchen, sipping a cup of tea that had long gone cold.

He'd been unable to sleep, tossing and turning so frequently that his wife, Sara, had kicked him out of bed. His insomnia was all because of his lack of progress on the Dorset theft case. Adrian West and Nick Harper, he was certain, had made progress.

Stevens had received a call from the police in Oxford after they'd chased down a man, James Poole, who'd committed suicide right in front of them. He hadn't been able to find out much about James Poole, at least not enough to link him to the stolen artifacts. He'd even gone to Oxford with Goode and Hawthorn to talk to the woman the street cameras had picked up Adrian and Nick visiting, Finlay Morrow, but her colleagues told them she'd abruptly taken a leave of absence.

He'd called Briggs to badger him about the whereabouts of his two agents. Briggs had reluctantly told him about the estate in Scotland they'd told him they were going to investigate; it had a link to James Poole. But he insisted that was the last he'd heard from them.

Stevens had followed the lead to Scotland, where the local police department had gone to the estate on his behalf, but found it empty. There was no sign of Grant Macleod, who was listed as the owner of the estate, nor anyone there. Macleod's trail had gone cold.

He now thoroughly regretted kicking Adrian and Nick off the case, but his bosses had been clear. There were those who were already skeptical of the unit's existence, and there was pressure to gain traction on the investigation. Any hint of witness harassment would have put a spotlight on their lack of progress; it would reek of desperation.

Still, he knew the move had been a mistake. Wherever they were, the two Americans had made far more progress than he had, which irritated him beyond measure. He'd also hoped that his knowledge of the Arthur legend, a topic his historian father had been obsessed with, would somehow help, but that knowledge had gotten him nowhere. Yet there had to be a link, as Finlay Morrow was a scholar of Arthurian legend.

Grant Macleod, Finlay Morrow . . . and Sorcha Manning. Another one of his regrets was believing Sorcha Manning, who'd also vanished. Doctor Manning had behaved too calmly for someone who'd been shot at. He suspected she was lying through her teeth when she'd promised to come to him if anyone else attempted to harm her. At the time, he hadn't suspected her because she had a clear alibi the night the artifacts were stolen, and a squeaky-clean background and reputation. Not tailing her when he'd had the chance was a grave mistake.

He set down his tea, rubbing his eyes, as his cell began to shrill. He stiffened, looking down at the number.

Speak of the devil. It was Sorcha Manning.

When he answered, however, it was Adrian West on the other end. As she spoke, his adrenaline rose, and the phone nearly dropped from his hand with all that she was telling him.

He was *definitely* not going to sleep tonight—or anytime soon.

CHAPTER 39

Two Days Later
Zvyozdochka, Sakha Republic
Russia
12:17 P.M.

Zvyozdochka, located in the Sakha Republic, was a town of only a few hundred that lay to the south of the Skalisty Range. The Sakha Republic, which covered the Siberia region, had one of the coldest climates in the world, with almost half of its territory lying above the Arctic Circle. Given its cold climate, vast size, and relative remoteness, it also had one of the lowest population densities in the world.

Zvyozdochka was now serving as the base camp for the dozens of law enforcement officials who had descended upon the town. They were using the local school gym, the only one in town, as their base of operations; the town's small police station couldn't hold everyone.

After Adrian had alerted DCI Stevens and then Briggs, they had launched into action, coordinating with several law enforcement departments all over the world—Scotland Yard, the FBI's field office in Moscow, and the Ministry of Internal Affairs of the Sakha Republic.

In an impressive forty-eight hours, officials from these departments had gathered here. Though there were some minor turf wars and personality clashes, everyone was intent on the same goal . . . locating the exact source of this biological weapon.

There was currently an APB out in several countries for Grant and Finlay. Stevens had initiated an internal review at Scotland Yard to seek out any officer who may have been compromised by Grant after Sorcha had given her reasons for not being truthful with him about the true nature of her involvement. To Adrian's relief, he hadn't been angry with them for staying on the case.

"It's a bloody good thing you did, given the progress you've made," Stevens had told them. "I apologize for what I said to you in the heat of anger, Adrian. It wasn't fair. I regretted kicking you off almost immediately, but I was beholden to my bosses."

Now, Adrian stood with Nick, Sorcha, Declan, and Stevens in front of a large map of the Skalisty mountain range. The local authorities had brought in a team of geologists who were familiar with the range. According to them, the most likely biological weapon that was hidden within these mountains was polonium, which could be extracted from uranium ore, plentiful in this region.

"What exactly is polonium?" Nick had asked.

"It's a radioactive element that's commonly used in nuclear weapons," one of the geologists, Pavel, informed him.

Adrian's heart had plummeted, and she locked eyes with Nick, Sorcha, and Declan, who had all gone pale at Pavel's words.

It now made sense to her. She could imagine an ancient tribe who lived in these remote mountains thousands of years ago, realizing that this region was dangerous when their people began dying, unbeknownst to them due to a radioactive substance. They had fled, getting as far away from the region as they could, gradually making their way west to Britain, with the shared memory of a place—a weapon—that could wipe out scores of people.

"Based on surveys, the places along the range with the highest concentration of uranium ore, and therefore polonium, is here, here, and here," Pavel said, pointing to several locations on the map. "We can send several survey teams out to these spots."

Adrian studied the map, hoping that one of these spots was accurate. What if Grant had already located the correct spot and had begun to mine? He certainly had the resources to do so. Pavel had told them all Grant needed to do was mine enough uranium ore to extract polonium, and then sell it at an incredibly high price on the black market.

Dread filled her at the thought. They didn't have a moment to spare.

Out of the corner of her eye, she spotted a local police officer hovering in the corner of the gym. She'd noticed that the young woman had tried to approach them several times, but her superior had stopped her each time.

Adrian could remember being the only woman in a male-dominated law enforcement department, and sympathy roiled through her. She wondered what the young woman wanted to tell them, and why her boss had repeatedly stopped her. If it was something that could get them closer to the location . . .

Adrian excused herself and approached the woman, who stiffened with surprise. Adrian offered her a warm smile. She spoke some Russian, and suspected that would endear herself to the young officer.

"Hi. I'm Adrian West," she said in Russian.

"I'm Tuyaara," Tuyaara replied, hesitantly returning her smile.

"I noticed there was something you seemed to want to tell us, but your boss wasn't allowing it," Adrian said. "Trust me, I was once the only woman in a department surrounded by men. I know what it's like."

Tuyaara's mouth tightened, but she gave her a sharp nod.

"You can tell me," Adrian encouraged her. "Anything can help us right now."

"When I heard about what you were looking for—a weapon—it made me think of stories passed down by my family. Tales of a tribe that once lived deep in the mountains, but they disappeared. The belief is that many of them died because of a curse, and the rest of them fled west, fleeing this curse."

Adrian studied Tuyaara, her mind racing. Local lore was often overlooked when it came to archaeological discoveries, and while a lot of myth and conjecture were added to such stories over the generations, they often possessed a core of truth.

"Did these tales mention a more precise location as to where this tribe once lived?" Adrian asked.

"Yes. A valley deep in the range, one that's barely—if ever—been explored because of its remoteness," Tuyaara replied.

"Can you point that area out on the map for the survey team?" Adrian asked, her heart picking up its pace.

CHAPTER 40

Skalisty Range
Sakha Republic, Russia
3:06 P.M.

The cold was so piercing that it cut into Adrian's bones.

Even with the layers of clothing and head-to-toe protective gear she wore, which consisted of a yellow radiation suit and plastic face shield equipped with a headlamp, she could feel the persistent chill. But she focused on putting one foot in front of the other as she made her way deeper into a remote valley in the Skalisty Range, along with Nick, Declan, Sorcha, and Tuyaara. They were trailing a three-person scientific-survey team led by Pavel, along with two local police officers.

Tuyaara's boss, Stevens, and the other authorities had been skeptical of Tuyaara's story, but Adrian had stood firm, insisting they at least check the location. They'd finally relented, agreeing to let Adrian and the others go with the scientific-survey team, along with two additional local police for extra security.

This part of the mountain range was so remote that a helicopter had to drop them off. The helicopter and the pilot were now parked a quarter of a mile behind them as they trudged farther into the valley.

A thick layer of snow covered the valley, and the mountains that surrounded them loomed ominously. Despite the imposing remoteness of the area, she could imagine a tribe settling here, using the cover of the mountains as a natural fortress. There were caverns cut into the mountainside that could also easily serve as habitable spaces. With a warmer climate thousands of years ago, this could have seemed like a promising home.

She could then see members of the tribe beginning to die of radiation poisoning, and without the scientific knowledge to understand why, the tribe then seeing this place as cursed, a deadly weapon, taking flight to the west, getting as far as they possibly could from this cursed place.

They soon reached the entrance to a cavern that cut into the side of the mountains, near the sloping edge of the valley. Pavel held up his Geiger counter, an electronic device he and the other geologists were using to detect radioactive material.

"I'm detecting high levels of radiation just beyond the entrance here," Pavel said. "Be very careful once we enter. Do not take off any of your protective gear, and try not to touch anything."

They nodded their agreement. Nervous anticipation hummed through Adrian. This could very well be the place the ancient tribe had encountered the radioactive material, the place whose location the brotherhood would hide and protect for centuries.

They made their way into the cavern, Pavel and the other two geologists leading the way. The cavern they entered was surprisingly deep, leading to a narrow, dark tunnel. They all flipped on their headlamps to guide their way, venturing even farther inside, until . . .

The ground began to rumble beneath their feet. Panicked, Adrian looked around, just as an explosion rocked the cavern, causing its entrance to violently tremble and cave in, as Adrian's world went black.

CHAPTER 41

Skalisty Range
Sakha Republic, Russia
3:22 P.M.

Grant felt the distant rumble of the explosion beneath his feet—and smiled.

He had to hand it to Finlay . . . she was brilliant. He cursed himself for keeping Sorcha alive when he had her. Finlay's expertise was more than enough.

She'd determined that the next tomb was at a church in Wales. He'd sent two of his mercenaries who were local to the area to the church to locate the old tomb and inscription, guided by Finlay. Finlay and two of his other experts had then brainstormed and analyzed all three inscriptions, with Finlay coming to the ultimate conclusion that the location they were looking for was in the mountains of Siberia.

Grant had contacts in Russia, mainly weapons dealers with whom he planned to do further business with once he had access to the weapon. They had put him in contact with a man, Mikhail who ran illegal mining operations throughout mountains of the region. With Mikhail's help, and the assistance of a local geologist he'd hired, it was determined exactly where the most likely location and source of the weapon was. Uranium ore, from which the deadly—and valuable—polonium could be extracted.

Excitement had hummed through his veins. He'd known that the biological weapon would prove valuable . . . he'd never imagined just how valuable.

Grant, Finlay, and several of his men had immediately flown privately from Manchester to Usta-Maya Airport in the Sakha Republic, where they met up with the mining team. For a cut of the proceeds, Mikhail had agreed to extract a certain amount of uranium ore that Grant could take out of the region.

The mining team had led him, Finlay and his men to a remote valley in the Skalisty Range. The team, who were used to dodging local authorities, had set up a booby-trapped explosive device by the main entrance in case the Americans and his niece and nephew were right behind them. There was a side exit to the mountainous caverns that they were going to use. A helicopter was at the ready nearby, waiting to transport Grant's team away from the mountains, along with the radioactive material from which they could extract the precious polonium.

Wearing protective gear, Grant, Finlay, and his men had accompanied the mining team deep into the caverns of the mountains, following long, winding tunnels that Finlay believed had been dug by the ancient tribe who'd once lived here. The geologist with the team had confirmed the high levels of uranium ore, and the team was in the process of extracting it for some time before the explosion rocked through the cavern.

Now, as the rumble of the explosion died down, he turned to his mercenaries.

"I want confirmation that whoever followed us is dead. And then we're taking what we've managed to extract so far and getting out of here."

3:25 P.M.

ADRIAN SLOWLY CAME TO, her ears ringing.

She lay sprawled out on the ground, surrounded by darkness. She shakily reached for her headlamp, flicking it on, and sitting up.

Nick was at her side, sitting up and looking dazed. Stark relief filled her at the sight of him, and she helped him to his feet.

Up ahead, she saw that Sorcha was partially trapped under rubble; Declan was already at her side, frantically removing rocks. Pavel and Inessa, another one of the geologists, lay eerily still, as did one of the police officers, Stepan. The force of the explosion had thrown them clear across the cavern. They were now slumped at the base of the left cavern wall.

Tuyaara was helping up the other police officer and scientist, Lev and Konstantin. Konstantin cradled his arm, which looked broken.

Adrian and Nick hurried forward, checking the pulses of Pavel, Inessa, and Stepan. Adrian closed her eyes, a heaviness settling over her . . . they were dead. It was all a matter of luck; the survivors had been farther inside the cavern, while Pavel, Inessa and Stepan were closer to the entrance when the explosion went off.

Adrian and Nick rushed toward Sorcha and Declan, helping him clear away the rest of the rubble that had trapped Sorcha. When they freed her, Adrian could see that Sorcha's leg was badly mangled; she let out a whimper of pain.

"It must have been an explosive booby trap," Lev said from behind them. "It's a common tool used by illegal miners."

Dread swirled in Adrian's belly. *Illegal miners.* That could only mean one thing. Once again, Grant had beaten them. He was here.

Adrian turned to look at the entrance, which had caved in. They were trapped. She didn't know if the pilot of the helicopter had heard the explosion from where he was waiting, but she could see that Lev was already reaching for his radio to call for help.

She stiffened when she heard footsteps jogging toward them from farther inside the cavern. It was likely the men who'd set up the explosive device coming to check their handiwork . . . and to finish the job.

They had to act fast.

Adrian turned, looking at the spot where she and Nick had landed after the explosion. Behind that area was the narrow entrance to another tunnel. She didn't know if it was an escape route, but it was a place to retreat.

"We have to hide until we figure out how to get out of here," she hissed. "*Fast*."

Moving quickly, Declan helped Sorcha up, hefting her into his arms. They all darted into the tunnel, scrambling away from the advancing footsteps.

The tunnel was even darker than the cavern, and Adrian was grateful for their headlamps. Up ahead, there was an opening, but it led to a yawning chasm several feet below.

Adrian halted in her tracks, horror seizing her. The others stopped around her, taking in the sight before them. Sorcha let out a soft gasp.

The chasm was full of bones. It looked like a mass grave. The ancient tribe who once dwelled here must have buried their dead in this place.

Behind them, she could hear the footsteps entering the tunnel and racing toward them.

There was no way out.

Adrian turned to the others, her mind racing. "I have an idea."

CHAPTER 42

3:29 P.M.

*A*drian, Declan, Nick, and Tuyaara sat crouched by the entrance of the chasm that led to the pit of bones, their pistols at the ready as the footsteps grew closer and closer.

Adrian's heart was in her throat, adrenaline pumping through her veins. She hoped that she'd made the right call with her plan. *This has to work.*

Adrian had told the others to let their pursuers come to them. The chasm of bones would take care of the rest. Given that there was no time to waste, no one had argued with her, quickly getting into position.

Sorcha, Konstantin, and Lev were hiding in one corner of the chasm, behind a small pile of bones. Given that both Sorcha and Konstantin were injured, Lev had agreed to stay with them as a safeguard; he would also radio for help once the coast was clear. Declan had reluctantly left Sorcha to Lev's protection; she knew the only reason he was coming with them was to go after his uncle.

Now, Adrian held her breath as the footsteps grew even closer, so close that she could hear the rapid breaths of the men behind their protective face shields.

Adrian and the others held still, until four men raced inside, clad in protective gear and fully armed.

Only then did Adrian spring to her feet, firing shots at the men as they neared the edge of the chasm. Nick, Tuyaara, and Declan followed suit, firing at the startled men, who fell into the chasm of bones with startled cries.

Adrian peered over the edge. The men lay still and unmoving on top of the bones below. Lev emerged from his hiding spot, helping Sorcha and Konstantin out as well. He gave them a nod, again turning on his radio to call for help. Adrian didn't know how long it would take for help to arrive once Lev made contact, but they couldn't afford to wait.

Adrian, Nick, and the others turned and headed out, racing back down the tunnel in the direction the men came from—the direction she believed would certainly lead to Grant. Grant and whoever he was with had to have an alternate way out of these mountains, otherwise they wouldn't have booby-trapped the entrance. They needed to find him, not only to make their own exit, but to stop him from leaving with any radioactive material that his men had extracted.

They moved at a run, using their headlamps to guide them through the darkness of the tunnel. Adrian clutched her pistol at her side, tense and on sharp alert, her breathing thunderous in her own ears. A steady hum of panic coursed through her. What if they were too late? What if Grant had already escaped?

They made their way past the caved-in entrance to the tunnel they'd heard the men coming from. The tunnel eventually led to an open area . . . filled with mining equipment.

Adrian's heart lurched. Grant's men had been here, and it was clear they had managed to extract some material. Even if it were a small amount, from what she'd learned from the geologists back at the base camp, it didn't take much polonium to make a nuclear weapon.

Panic gripped her once again. Were they already too late?

"Adrian," Nick said, pointing at the ground. He'd aimed his headlight at the ground, which bore multiple sets of boot prints, leading out of the open area to yet another tunnel.

They followed the prints into the tunnel, taking off at a run, moving as fast as they could beneath the weight of their protective gear, until they reached a massive cavern that plummeted into a dark, yawning chasm below, its walls and ceiling filled with jagged, pike-shaped rocks.

A rocky natural bridge stretched across the chasm to the other side of the cavern, where Adrian could see several forms clad in protective gear, carefully making their way along the rocky edge toward an exit on the far end of the cavern. Though he was covered in gear, she recognized one of the tall forms as Grant's, and the smaller form next to him as Finlay. Both of them were carrying medium-sized metal boxes.

Her adrenaline surged. Exchanging a look with Nick, Adrian and the others darted across the rocky bridge toward Grant.

Grant's men spotted them and whirled, firing multiple shots. Adrian returned fire, along with Nick and the others, as they continued to race across the bridge, dodging the bullets coming their way.

Adrian realized in a panic that the bridge they were crossing was growing increasingly shaky, and she heard the groaning sound of crumbling rock.

The bridge they were on was falling out from beneath them.

"RUN!" she screamed.

CHAPTER 43

*A*drian and Nick dashed toward the end of the bridge, Declan and Tuyaara on their heels. She and Nick made it to the other side, turning to pull Tuyaara in as she joined them. But the bridge crumbled right beneath Declan's feet, and he started to plummet—

Adrian lunged forward, Nick grasping on to her waist, grabbing Declan's hands before he could fall. Using their joint strength, Adrian, Nick, and Tuyaara pulled Declan up until he was safely on the other side.

They moved quickly, scrambling to their feet and racing down the same narrow bridge along the cavern's edge that Grant and the others had taken, which led to an exit to another tunnel. But this time, Adrian could glimpse light ahead. An exit to the outside.

She picked up her pace, and they dashed

toward the light. She saw the outline of Grant and the other figures as they raced toward it.

Adrian ran as fast as she could, desperate to not lose him. She was certain that he had some method of escape. They couldn't let him leave.

As they drew close to the exit, terror bloomed in her chest. She could see that both sides of the exit had been rigged with explosive devices. They must be similar to the ones planted near the main entrance . . . that was why Grant's men had stopped firing at them. They had another—more efficient method—of killing them.

She saw one of Grant's men turn as they cleared the exit, lifting a detonator.

Sprinting forward, Nick at her side, they both fired multiple shots at the man, who crumpled to the ground before he could set it off.

Adrian and the others darted out of the exit, which led out to a narrow mountain pass. In the near distance, Adrian could hear the whirring blades of a helicopter.

Grant was making his escape.

Grant and Finlay were rushing down the pass, trailed by their men.

Grant's men whirled, raising their weapons to fire. Adrian and Nick fired, along with Tuyaara and Declan, continuing to charge forward as the men crumpled.

Adrian and Nick sprinted forward. She could see the helicopter, which now hovered at the edge of the mountain pass, lowering a ladder. Finlay was already climbing it.

In spite of everything, Adrian didn't want to do this, but she had no choice. She raised her weapon, aiming it at Finlay.

But gunfire erupted from the helicopter, aimed directly at them. Adrian and the others dove to the ground, returning fire. Fury and terror filled Adrian as Finlay safely climbed into the helicopter.

Grant began to climb the ladder. Keeping low, she and Nick crawled forward, using the surrounding rocks of the mountain pass to shield them, firing multiple shots at Grant. One of their bullets caught him in the leg, and he tumbled to the ground with a cry.

The helicopter lifted into the air, turning to fly away.

Frustration and despair filled her; she could only pray that the police and rescue helicopters headed their way would intercept it.

"I'm on it," Tuyaara said, as if reading her mind, taking out her radio, her eyes on the helicopter as if flew away.

Adrian rushed forward, aiming her pistol at Grant, who was clutching his bleeding leg, his face taut with pain.

"It's over," she said.

Grant opened his mouth to respond, but a voice from behind her halted him.

"Uncle Grant."

She turned. Declan stood there, aiming his own weapon at Grant, his expression hard.

"She's right. This isn't our family's legacy. The brotherhood's legacy."

Fury contorted Grant's features. "Our family has become *weak*. That's why I got rid of them, they left me with no choice. I had hope for you, but you turned out to be just as weak."

Adrian stiffened with surprise at the revelation. At her side, she could see Declan's reaction—grief, horror, shock. His eyes filled with tears and his finger trembled on the trigger.

"Declan," Adrian said. "We have him. There's no need."

Grant glared at Declan, as if challenging him. Adrian focused on Declan; she needed to reach him. "You said it yourself. This is not what the brotherhood—what your family's legacy—was about."

Her words seemed to reach him. Declan lowered his weapon.

Adrian and Nick moved toward Grant, but Grant lifted his arm, revealing a pistol he had hidden.

It happened fast.

Grant aimed his pistol at Declan, his face contorted with rage, hefting himself up on his injured leg. But his grip on the mountain rock was precarious, and his other leg caught on a patch of ice on the edge of the narrow pass.

He teetered as Adrian, Nick, and Declan raced forward . . . but it was already too late.

Grant tumbled over the edge of the mountain pass, plunging to his death.

CHAPTER 44

Zvyozdochka, Sakha Republic
Russia
7:37 *P.M.*

Adrian made her way outside of the school that was serving as the base camp for law enforcement, hunkering into the warmth of her parka as she watched several helicopters make their way north toward the Skalisty Range.

A police helicopter had intercepted the helicopter that had flown Finlay away; she and the men aboard were all now in custody. A separate rescue team had arrived not long after Grant's fall from the mountain pass; the team had transported Sorcha and Konstantin to a local hospital. Declan had accompanied his sister.

The rescuers had transported Adrian, Nick, Tuyaara, and Lev back to the base camp, where Stevens and the local authorities had questioned them extensively. They'd then debriefed with Briggs via a video call. Tuyaara was now with her colleagues and superior, giving them a separate debriefing. Since they'd returned to base camp, Tuyaara was now getting the respect she deserved from her colleagues, even if it was grudging.

The authorities had sealed off the section of the mountain where they'd found the mass grave and illegal mining site. Various local and international agencies were being helicoptered in to take control of the site for protection and containment. One geologist at the base camp had informed Adrian that from their initial readings, the polonium within the uranium ore in the mountains had an even higher concentration than normal, making it even more dangerous. Dread filled Adrian at the thought of what could have happened had Grant been able to mine and extract large amounts of the deadly material.

The door swung open behind Adrian, and Nick joined her, tucking his gloved hands into the pockets of his parka.

"Why couldn't this place have been in the Mediterranean or Caribbean somewhere?" he grumbled. "Remind me to never complain about winters in DC again."

Adrian smiled as Nick fell silent, following her gaze to the mountains in the distance.

"Can you imagine?" he asked, his tone serious now. "Living in a place that you think is safe, only to watch your people die . . . and to have no idea what caused it? To have knowledge of such a deadly place and keep it secret for generations?"

Adrian shook her head, watching the imposing mountains, thinking of the people who had once lived here and drifted west, eventually arriving in the British Isles. Admiration swelled over her at the thought of their selflessness and determination. They could have used such a secret to their own gain, but they had chosen not to, knowing the destructive power that lay in these mountains.

"So," Nick said, forcing her back to the present. "Do you really want to go back to life as a boring old professor? I just got off another call with Briggs. He told me you're welcome to join the bureau in whatever capacity you want." He studied her for a long moment. "What's it going to be, West? Have you decided?"

Adrian looked at him and smiled.

"I have," she said simply.

CHAPTER 45

Two Weeks Later
FBI Headquarters
Washington, DC
11:37 A.M.

It felt strange to walk through FBI headquarters.

Years ago, she had walked out of these offices, bitter, broken and angry, determined never to return. Yet here she was, with Nick at her side, walking confidently back into the fire, with none of the weight from her past on her shoulders. Just an eagerness to move forward.

She'd known that this was the life for her the moment she'd accepted this case—hell, the moment she'd taken on the Cleopatra case. As much as she loved ancient languages and history, and would always have a foot in the world of academia through guest lectures, publishing, and conferences

... the world of investigation, adventure, and saving lives was in her bones. It was something she could no longer deny.

Now that she'd once again experienced the rush of solving an ancient mystery and saving lives in the process, she didn't see how she could go back to the life she thought she'd wanted. It was time to return to her true passion, the one she'd turned her back on out of misplaced frustration and anger. Her boss at the university had taken her resignation with grace, insisting that there was always an open door for her to return.

Adrian had worried there would be an enormous amount of press over what happened in Russia, akin to the attention she, Nick, and the others involved had received after the discovery of Cleopatra's tomb. But due to the dangerous nature of the discovery, it had been classified and the authorities kept it under wraps.

Even the stolen artifacts, which authorities had recovered from one of Grant's homes, were quietly returned to the British Museum without the usual press or fanfare. The sword had also been returned. A conservation team had carefully put the hilt back together after cataloguing the inscriptions. Separate archaeological teams had traveled to the churches in France and Wales to catalog and analyze the remnants of the tombs they'd found, along with the remains.

Sorcha was back working at the British Museum, using crutches until her leg fully healed.

Despite their rocky start, Adrian now considered Sorcha a friend, and they had promised to stay in touch. News of Michel's death had devastated Sorcha, and though she was still grieving, she was now the de facto leader of the brotherhood per his wishes. It was undergoing a gradual transformation into a historical society, with the approval of its legitimate members, now that its purpose had been fulfilled.

"And it probably shouldn't be called 'the brotherhood' anymore, now that a woman is leading it," Sorcha had told her with a chuckle.

Without Grant at the helm, his side of the brotherhood had dismantled, with members either under investigation, on the run from authorities, or leaving the brotherhood altogether.

As for Declan, he'd insisted on turning himself in for his part in the theft. Because of his cooperation, revealing all he knew about Grant and his crimes, his lawyer was in the process of working out a probation deal so that he wouldn't serve jail time.

Nick, who had come a long way from his initial distrust of Declan, had vouched for him, along with Adrian, telling Stevens that Declan had risked his life alongside them to take down his uncle once he realized what Grant's true intentions were. While Declan and Nick hadn't formed a friendship like the one Adrian had with Sorcha, they'd left Russia on good terms, and had even shaken hands before getting on separate flights out of the country.

"What can I say," Nick had said with a shrug.

"Declan and the rest of us survived an explosion in a Russian cave, an armed ambush in a French chateau and a Welsh church . . . events like that *kind of* forces you to set aside petty differences. We're like old war buddies now."

Declan was currently living with Sorcha in London while his probation was finalized, though Sorcha had jokingly told Adrian in her latest email that she was helping him get his own place. He'd reverted to his teenage tendencies of messiness and staying up at all hours of the night, blasting the television. But Adrian could tell that she was happy to have her brother back in her life.

Now, Adrian looked over at Nick, who gave her a wide grin. He was thrilled by her decision to return to the bureau and had pulled her into an embrace when she'd informed him of her decision to return. Warmth had filled her at his touch, and she'd welcomed the feeling.

Adrian looked forward to having Nick at her side again. She'd missed him more than she'd realized during their years apart. The flow of attraction still hummed between them, and what would become of that remained an open question.

They'd just come from having breakfast with her mother, who lived in nearby Alexandria. Adrian had worried about her mother's reaction to her decision, but she'd confirmed that she was happy with it.

"As much as I'll worry, traveling the world and

defeating bad guys is what you were always meant to do," she'd said.

Adrian and Nick had come into headquarters because Briggs wanted them to meet with him. Adrian had just applied for her reinstatement with the bureau shortly after returning to the US from Russia, and the process was still ongoing, so it surprised her that he wanted to meet so soon. Briggs was vague as to the exact reason for the meeting, but he did mention there was another case he wanted to talk to them about.

When she and Nick arrived at his office, Briggs ushered them inside. To her surprise, there were two men and a woman already gathered there. Briggs introduced them as representatives from the CIA, the Department of Defense, and Homeland Security.

Adrian and Nick exchanged a glance before taking a seat opposite them.

"First of all, congratulations. You've no doubt saved countless lives with your actions in Russia," Briggs said. "I've asked you here to let you in on something that's been in the works for some time. Art Crimes is often limited in its scope, and the higher-ups have wanted us to work jointly with other departments to broaden it. The FBI, CIA, and Homeland have recognized threats here and abroad related to relics and stolen artifacts that terrorists want to exploit for their own means, and we want a specialized team to take on such threats." Briggs leaned forward, his gaze serious. "Given your very successful track record with such threats in such a short amount of time, we want you both as leads on this, with a support team, led by Vince, to work with you."

Astonishment filled Adrian, but also a rush of excitement. At her side, Nick also looked stunned.

"Before you give me your answer, you should know what the first case we'd like you to take on involves. It may sound . . . a little out there at first, but we have credible intelligence coming from Greece regarding this."

Adrian leaned forward in her chair, her curiosity burning. "What does it involve?"

Briggs glanced over at the other officials before returning her gaze.

"Atlantis."

∼

The adventure continues in Book Three, THE ATLANTIS CONSPIRACY. Start reading now!

THE ATLANTIS CONSPIRACY

A lost city. An ancient conspiracy. A deadly countdown to mass annihilation...

When an ancient papyrus linked to the lost city of Atlantis is stolen, Adrian West and Nick Harper are summoned to Athens to assist in the investigation.

But they soon find themselves in a lethal game of cat and mouse with members of a shadowy yet powerful organization intent on finding the ruins of Atlantis for their own deadly means...

From the streets of Athens to the ruins of ancient societies on islands that dot the Mediterranean, Adrian must prevent a secret that lies with Atlantis from causing modern day destruction that would annihilate billions...

Start reading now!

AUTHOR'S NOTE

The genesis of the idea for this novel began with two questions.

Was the legendary King Arthur real?

And if so, who was he based upon?

My research to answer this question led me not to medieval England, as the Disney film and many Arthurian portrayals have depicted, but to an earlier time, in the fifth century. Sub-Roman Britain, the period right after Rome's legions left Britannia, their name for Britain, to return to Rome and fight the various invaders that would ultimately sack the Roman Empire.

The people left behind in Britain had formed a Romano-British identity, but were now quite literally left on their own to fight off the invading Saxons, Picts, and other tribes. This is the start of Europe's Dark Ages, and it's when Arthur's legend takes root.

There are several likely inspirations for a histor-

AUTHOR'S NOTE

ical King Arthur, I chose three based on the similarity of their lives and deaths in relation to the legendary Arthur. Owain Danwyn, Ambrosius Aurelanius and Riothamus are actual historical figures, though not much is known about them. The one thing they have in common, and what links them to the legendary Arthur, is their fending off barbarian armies on behalf of Rome or the Romano-British.

While the specific Ogham inscriptions—and the sword—mentioned in this novel are fictional, Ogham inscriptions do exist and have been found all over the United Kingdom, primarily in Britain, Ireland and Wales.

The brotherhood mentioned in this novel is my invention, in addition to the tombs found by Adrian and the others. No one knows where these historical "Arthurs" are buried, though there are theories. The strongest one is for Owain Danwyn, whom the historian Geoffrey Ashe believes—with compelling evidence—is buried in the Berth Hill complex, which I discuss further below.

The villages and cities mentioned in this novel all exist and are real places, however, I did take some liberties. Avallon, France, Baschurch, England, and Dinas Mawddwy, Wales all exist, with ties to the Arthur legend. While the Berth Hill complex exists, it's on private land and not open to the public, so the Berth Hill Museum and Historical Society is my invention. The actual local

AUTHOR'S NOTE

museum dedicated to Berth Hill is in Shrewsbury, England.

Christian churches were commonly built over pagan temples, something done all over Europe during the gradual conversion to Christianity from pagan practices.

The hillock Sorcha takes Grant and Finlay to, the Bassa Hills, and remnants of a pagan temple, is fictional. Additionally, the name of the hills, Abas Hills, that Adrian and the team go to in Wales is fictional (the actual name of the hills in the area is called Dyfi Hills), but the village and the three rivers that form a junction there are real places.

The notion of Excalibur being a place is also my invention. There is, however, genetic evidence for peoples migrating from the Pontic Steppe ending up in Ireland, specifically the blood disorder found in Ireland known as the "Celtic disease". There is also evidence for a lingering Celtic presence in the east; the links the Ossetian tribe have to the Celts is based in fact, including the typically Celtic spiral found in some of their designs, the reverential use of oak, and the "round tables" found in Ossetian homes.

As for the final location in Siberia, the Skalisty Mountain Range does exist, but it is incredibly remote and isolated, and has only been surveyed—barely—in the early twentieth century. The Russian region is one that has the highest concentration of uranium ore, which makes the Skalisty

AUTHOR'S NOTE

Range an ideal location for the "place" that is the ultimate weapon.

A bit of a scientific note. Polonium, a deadly material that is used in nuclear weapons, actually exists in a relatively small proportion to uranium ore. An average of one hundred micrograms of polonium are found in one ton of uranium ore, so in reality it's not economically viable to extract polonium from uranium ore. (For this reason, polonium is usually created in a nuclear reactor using a stable isotope called bismuth-209.) I took liberties for the sake of this novel, giving the polonium discovered in the Skalisty Range a much higher concentration than it would actually have.

I used many resources in my research for this novel, from an array of scientific and historical articles to nonfiction books. Several of my most helpful resources—and excellent, fascinating reading—include *The Discovery of King Arthur* by Geoffrey Ashe, *The Lost Tomb of King Arthur* by Graham Phillips, and *King Arthur* by Christopher Hibbert.

I hope you've enjoyed Adrian's adventure! Her adventure continues with one of the most enduring and fascinating ancient mysteries ... the lost city of Atlantis.

Until next time,
—L.D.G.
2022

ABOUT THE AUTHOR

L.D. Goffigan writes fast-paced thrillers and action-adventure with historical intrigue. She studied film and dramatic writing at New York University and currently divides her time between France and California.

When not writing, you can find her traveling to places she's never been, reading the latest book which strikes her fancy, or watching a documentary about ancient mysteries.

To be notified about new releases, visit L.D. Goffigan's website to join her newsletter. Subscribers are also alerted to giveaways and exclusive bonus content.

Stay in touch!
ld@ldgoffiganbooks.com
ldgoffiganbooks.com

www.ingramcontent.com/pod-product-compliance
Lightning Source LLC
LaVergne TN
LVHW041905070526
838199LV00051BA/2497